Jewel Time

By

Kenneth M. Lee

Jewel Time

The third book of the Marcia Lane Suspense Stories
By Kenneth M. Lee

Copyright ©2023Kenneth M. Lee
ISBN 9780971185081

Printed in the United States of America

This is a work of fiction.

Names, characters, places, and incidences are purely the works of imagination, though a few of the physical locations in the Tidewater area are real. But any resemblance to actual persons, living or dead, businesses, offices, companies, and events, are purely coincidental.

Kenneth M. Lee
1382 Grandpa Ln., Loris SC 29569
E-Mail: kenlwor@gmail.com
Blog: http://thedivineway.wordpress.com

Dedication

To all Native Americans and their descendants.

1.

Jim Cloudwaters and his mother Emma Rivers approached Ward's Furniture Store on Main Street walking slowly in the midst of a fog that had covered the Peninsula section of Virginia for two days.

It wasn't unusual for warm air to arrive in the spring and meet the cool waters of the Chesapeake to create fog, but here at 10:00a.m., fog had usually burned off from a sun that had no barriers on this coastal land.

A chest of drawers in the display window at Wards caught Jim's attention.

1

He looked quizzically at the pieces of wood that had been put together to make the chest and said, "From our trees, they show off the woods and make money."

Emma nodded her head while realizing the hurt and pain her son felt from years of disrespect and disparagement being an Indian: he was always the last person chosen for school activities, medical attention, and transportation needs.

Jim and Emma were members of the Powhatan.

After the Powhatan had been moved from their pristine grounds by the white man's "deed paper genocide", they found themselves on shifting pieces of mud flats fronting the James River.

But few people knew then the primitive value of the flats: they were prime areas for shell fishing.

At least they were away from the hustle and bustle of traffic, crime, and raucous soldiers from nearby military installations who often partied all weekend.

But their 30-acre plot of scrub brush, marsh, and wetlands, with a small cabin on it, was now being isolated from access by a locked gate. And Jim had no idea who was locking it.

Other Indians talked of the same thing happening to them throughout the country: someone was locking gates in and around the perimeter of their lands.

"They've always had the bigger guns," the old people would say to Jim and his parents.

But Jim believed there could be a civil way to enjoy what he owned. After all, his family was here first.

Jim and Emma continued walking past the picture window and came to a metal framed door that said "Stronger's Investigative Service".

They looked at each other and nodded in agreement. Jim opened the door and they walked up the stairs to another door.

They looked at the lettering on the door, and it matched the lettering on the downstairs door and on a card that Private Investigator Marcia Lane had left in their cabin months earlier when she had visited and wanted information about their non-profit organization which was protesting a cell phone tower installation. Marcia was curious about the group that was standing up to the telecom companies.

After nodding to each other again, Emma put the card back in her wallet and looked suspiciously at Jim.

Indians would never do anything in a hurry when it came to dealing with white people.

She would never trust the white people again after unwanted roads were made on her property, receiving mail that threatened her with eviction, and strange people trespassing with rods, scopes, and lines of string.

But Jim had persuaded her to come. He said they needed help and must learn to work with the whites -- since they were here and weren't going anywhere.

Jim took off his black felt hat that had a blue jay's feather on it. Both were wet, and he shook the rain off the hat's brim.

He himself was hesitant about entering the door and giving away secrets only the Indians knew about his land and business.

He brushed some rain off his black leather coat and straightened his necklace -- which had a black megalodon shark's tooth hanging at its bottom.

The tooth had been found just off the shoreline of the York River when Jim was a young kid. Had not the sun been shining on its enameled surface, he never would have seen it in the mud.

But there it was: a 3" triangular black enameled pointed tooth with serrated root lines at its top.

Jim thought it must have been a big shark, but another man told him of a 7" tooth, 2" thick, that had been found. But the man had traded it in exchange for food years earlier.

Jim was proud of his shark's tooth, and he wore it daily. With a gold wire wrapped around its top and hanging from a black leather cord, it was a sight to behold, and a good conversation piece.

For one thing, no one had touched it but him: it was something God had created and no white man had polluted it.

Emma stomped her feet on the straw pad in front of the door as if giving a warning that she was in no mood to play around.

Jim stomped his too, and they both smiled at each other and laughed.

He knocked on the door lightly and opened it to see Marcia Lane and Rufus Stronger sitting at two separate desks hunched over and looking at papers.

Marcia was looking at the latest crime report in the city of Newport News while Rufus was verifying hours spent spying on a politician's wife.

Marcia recognized Emma immediately from their meeting months earlier and said, "Welcome to *my* office".

Rufus knew of the two Indians but looked on as a stranger would. Finally, he welcomed the two and asked if they'd like some coffee.

Emma spoke up and said, "Two cups. Pure".

Rufus in his country twang said, "As pure as Folgers makes it."

He walked over to a stand and poured two cups of coffee and brought them to Jim and Emma.

Emma nodded her head and walked towards Marcia while shifting her shoulders and letting Jim take off her olive-drab mackintosh coat.

She sat down in a chair in front of Marcia's desk and brought her leather purse to her lap. She took out Marcia's card and laid it on the desk and said, "You forgot this."

Marcia had been humbled once in front of Emma -- feeling guilt and shame of being party to ethnic robbing of Indian land.

She nodded her head and said, "Yes."

Jim spoke up and introduced himself, and he found a chair near the window and sat. He would never allow any white person to walk behind him; besides, he liked a bird's-eye view of downtown outside the window.

Marcia was wondering what had brought the two Indians here.

She knew Jim Cloudwaters was a member of a group that was protesting cell phone tower installations and helping an accused Indian man who was unfairly charged with murder. She also knew, from her boyfriend Richie, that Jim had access to lots of money.

So she relaxed, and in a business-like manner said. "Well, it's good to see you two. What can we do for you?"

Rufus just smiled, taking in the scene with his usual diminutive manner.

Emma looked at Rufus and shifted a little in her seat --exposing her colored woolens that covered her legs under a jaded cotton pullover dress that had a small gold crucifix hanging down her chest.

She was a beautiful old woman -- the kind of woman whose jet set black eyes spoke of wisdom and kindness -- though her brown face was aged from hard work and worry.

Jim sipped his coffee and found it good. He smiled and nodded his head as he sipped the warm liquid.

Then he set the cup down on the windowsill and looked briefly to the street below; then to the sky above where the rainy mist had been replaced by rays of sunshine and blue skies.

He looked at Marcia and Rufus and said, "We have a problem on our land."

"What kind of problem?" Marcia asked.

"There is a trespasser who keeps locking us out."

"That's been going on a long time, hasn't it?"

Jim knew Marcia would understand, and that's why he was here "You bet, from the beginning."

Rufus said, "Seems like those treaties signed long ago allowed each other to go across each other's lands."

"Well, that's true," said Jim. "But when someone puts up a gate up and locks it, can't no one go across it but the person with the key."

"Be good if the land was deeded," Rufus said, wanting to make sure Jim's land was deeded and that he understood about land registration in a white man's world.

"Well, we've got our land, but there were too many Chiefs and not enough Indians."

"Oh," Rufus said as he nodded his head and smiled.

Jim continued on: "You see. That's just it. Treaties were made for access to each other's land but the whites made encroachments to their liking and claimed lands under squatter's rights."

"They do that," Rufus said.

"Our acreage along the James River is ours because we were there first, and some of us have stayed there. Where are our squatter's rights?"

"You may need a lawyer for that."

Marcia looked on with her chin resting on her right hand and the newspaper still open on the desk.

"They don't recognize us as a people. We're not on the birth records! Some man in Richmond at that Bureau of Statistics office labeled Indian newborns as either black or white – there weren't no box for "Indian"."

"Well, who do you think is trespassing?" Rufus asked.

"Don't know. That's why we've come here asking for help."

"Okay. We can do that," and he looked at Marcia for agreement.

"Are there any special times you find the gate locked?" Marcia asked, looking at Jim.

"Usually on weekends, or after we leave the compound for the day," Jim said.

9

"So, how do you get access?"

"We use bolt cutters."

Emma sat and listened intently while finishing the last of her coffee.

"And where is your land?"

"Right behind where you were at -- north on the James River from where the boats first landed and where it's always been. Diggers often come around the old fort at Jamestown looking at our road. You'll see the gate on the right."

"Can I see it from the river?"

"Yes."

Marcia looked at Rufus and said, "May have to go fishing."

2.

"Well, that's not all," Jim said.

Marcia looked on intently knowing that there was more to this complaint than about someone trespassing.

"People have been following us," Jim said.

Rufus, in his sublime way, got up slowly from his desk and walked over to the coffee machine to make sure it was unplugged. He hitched his trousers and checked for his gun at his rear. He then walked over to the window near Jim.

Jim moved a little being surprised.

11

But Rufus was there to look out the window and at the street below.

"You see them, Jim?" Marcia asked as she knew what Rufus was doing.

"Yeah. Two men. One was older with gray hair and sunglasses on all the time. The other about 40. Both dressed nice. On three occasions."

Rufus looked out the window and said, "There are two men." He was looking at a black sedan parked on the street in front of Rosie's Cafe just below the office.

"A black sedan, Jim?" Rufus asked.

"Yes."

"Need a tag number."

"I'll go get it Rufus," Marcia said.

"No. They'll be gone. They're looking at the front door of the entrance. But at least get a picture."

Marcia grabbed the bigger camera in her desk drawer, a Nikon with a long lens. She walked over to the window and gave the camera to Rufus and said, "Here. You take the picture. I'll be right back."

Rufus gave her a double look and turned the camera on shielding it from the rays of sunshine that were now streaming through the window.

Marcia walked over to the bathroom area and let her hair down from its bun wrap that was on top of her head. She walked around the bathroom door, shed her navy ribbed top sweater, and put on a white buttoned-up sweater with the top button undone. She combed her blonde wavy hair and let it hang loosely over her shoulders and front -- shook her head from side to side -- and frizzled it slightly.

The sun was shining but she grabbed her umbrella anyway. If anything, it would afford protection if she needed it. Besides, its navy blue color went well with her pants.

She gave a big smile to the three of them and walked out the door and down the steps to street level and opened the door slowly smiling with a carefree walk.

She crossed the street to where the sedan was parked.

"Look, that's not the Indian woman," Reginald Fuzman said as he looked intently at Marcia who had come out the office entrance door and was walking towards them.

"Let's get out of here. It's probably Marcia Lane the investigator and we don't need no part of her," Brent McDougall said.

"No. Look at her. She's pretty."

"Yeah, and she's coming this way."

"Just another sec or two. I ain't never seen an investigator woman."

Brent started the engine of the late model Crown Victoria and looked around to see that the car was nearly trapped, and as fast as Marcia was walking, he was sure his license tag would be noticed.

He put the car in reverse and backed up to the car in the rear. He quickly turned onto the street speeding by the quick-paced Marcia who had now stopped and stared at him and Jack in the car.

"That's it Jack. She's got us. Now we got to get the garage man to change the license plate."

"No problem. We got an alias on this plate."

"The number CIA-119 is not going to go over well."

"I thought it was supposed to intimidate people."

"People? Fine. But that's Marcia Lane, and she knows what is happening."

"Sure was pretty."

"Yeah. Well you can look at her picture in the newspaper while you're sitting in jail."

Marcia memorized the license plate number and buttoned her top together. She smiled and she waved to

Jim, Rufus, and Emma, who were watching from the 2nd floor window.

"Wow. What a woman!" Jim said.

"Knew there was a reason why I hired her," Rufus murmured as he went back to his chair with the camera and looked at the pictures he had taken.

Emma, who hardly says anything, said, "I like her."

"What will happen now?" Jim asked.

"Got to find out who was in the car," Rufus said. "They don't look like trespassers but they sure act like guilty ones."

"No. They sit back a ways from the access road and let someone else do the walking to lock the gate I suppose."

"I see. Okay, Jim. We'll be in touch with you. See what we can find out. Just go about your normal day."

"Thank you."

"Hey. Have you reported this to the local police?"

"That's who is in the car."

Rufus eyebrows shot up.

"The one driving. When I was going to the store the other day, he drove beside me real slow and I looked over to see who it was. It was the same man driving the black car but with a police uniform on."

"Okay. That makes it easier."

Marcia came into the office with that same smile on her face.

"Got it boss."

"You did. If I did that, they would have done a u-turn and been gone before I could get it."

"Every man needs a woman."

"Glad I got you."

Emma rose slowly and put her empty cup on Marcia's desk. She gathered her coat from the coat rack hanger, and Jim walked over to help her.

They both said bye and left Rufus and Marcia staring at each other.

"Sounds like a good job to me," Rufus said.

Marcia chuckled and said, "Anything's better than being on the water looking for clams this time of year."

3.

"Jim said the driver in the car was driving a police car the other day," Rufus said as Marcia was dressing back into her daily work wear.

"Well, Captain Tellis should know the guy," she yelled from behind the bathroom door as she brushed her hair back over her navy sweater and looked at herself in the mirror.

"We won't contact him right now – see what these devils do. Maybe go see Baily at the west side crime sector and see what he knows."

"Sounds good. I'll be ready in a second."

"We'll run the plate later."

Rufus stepped away from his desk but then reached back to retrieve a case for the bullets in his pistol.

"Can't go to Bailys loaded," he muttered, "so leave your gun."

Marsha heard every word as she exited the bathroom area and said, "Okay. How about a knife?"

"Might get away with that."

"Actually, a little lip gloss, eye shadow, and perfume would help."

"Works every time."

They locked up the office and went downstairs to the parking lot and got in Rufus' Toyota.

Rufus drove through town to a nightclub on the west side of town and stopped in a no parking zone. He sat for a minute looking the area over.

Marcia knew what he was doing but nevertheless said, "Could get towed from here."

"It would take awhile, and I got insurance."

"Yeah, but I get off in a few hours and have dinner planned."

18

"Well, in that case, we ought to move. Been long enough anyway for someone to report us and send a policeman."

"Rufus, you are one smart cookie."

"Better than being a doughnut with a hole in it."

Rufus parked the Toyota in a vacant spot and they both walked across the street and down an alley until they came to a door with a green light over it.

Rufus knocked three times, two times, and then a loud one time. He knew the code.

Big Nort opened the door slowly and saw Rufus.

"Rufus."

"Nort."

Nort looked around to see Marcia standing behind Rufus.

"You got angel face with you."

"Is. She's my protector."

"Right pretty protector. What you want?"

"Looks can be deceiving. Baily in?"

"Depends."

"He owes me one."

"He does."

Nort opened the door wider only to have his partner Red step in and block the way with his hands stretched out.

"Need to check them Nort. You know that."

"We come unloaded," Rufus said as he waited.

"Except for her," Red said as he smiled and got a whiff of Marcia's perfume.

"Boss don't like meetings without a notice," Red said.

Red looked at Nort and nodded okay.

Red stepped aside to let Rufus and Marcia walk down an unlighted hallway to an open doorway and elongated room. Baily was playing solitaire on a mahogany table in a large concrete enclosed room with his back to the wall. He had a cigarette in his mouth and looked up at the group.

"Well, well, well. If it ain't water boy and his new girlfriend," Baily said as he continued laying down cards.

Rufus nodded toward Marcia and said, "This is Marcia Lane."

"Pretty partner, and mean from what I hear."

Baily put his cards down and sat back blowing smoke rings in front of him.

"I don't like uninvited guests in my office," he said.

Marcia said, "Neither do I," speaking of Red and Nort and how they barged in her office one day.

"Now what do you two want?"

"Need a favor."

"I gather that, but okay, since you told me last month about Mr. Osmond who was tapping into my territory."

"Big black Crown following my two Indian clients around the area and one was a policeman."

Marcia flipped open a gallery of photos from a tablet that had the Nikon SD card in it and showed him the picture of the car and its occupants.

"That is Reginald Fuzman in the passenger seat. Don't know the other guy," Baily said as he looked over the picture.

"Why would Fuzman be following two Indians?"

"Well, I don't rightly know, but Fuzman ain't no policeman. He could be portraying a policeman, That does happen. Put on a cap with a badge, a magnetic sign on the door, and there's your policeman."

"Maybe. What else is Fuzman?" Marcia asked.

"Reggie steals jewelry, antiques, and archaeological shards."

That was enough for Rufus to hear: he turned around to see if Nort and Red were behaving. Nort stood at the door while Red was leaning against a sidewall.

"Well, that explains that. How's things going with you?" Rufus asked.

"Same old stuff. Horny G.I.'s from the base, a few foreigners from the freighters, and there's always a little trading going on with low taxes next door in Carolina."

"Business is good then," Rufus said.

"Is what it is," Baily said.

"Thanks a lot Baily. You've been a big help."

"Anytime big man. Take care of pretty thing there."

Nort and Red moved out of the way to let Rufus and Marcia leave.

Marcia didn't look at either of them but stayed close to Rufus as they walked out of the bulding to the Toyota.

Now they had a fresh new outlook as to why Jim and Emma were being stalked.

And it certainly wasn't over land.

4.

After Rufus and Marcia got into the Toyota and Rufus had turned onto the road, he spoke up and said, "Well. What do you think?"

"I think Jim and Emma are hiding something besides someone trespassing on their land. I mean, why would a jewel thief and some dude with a 119 License number be cajoling around them?"

"Unless there was something very valuable on that land."

"No doubt. But there's another person somewhere, probably at the cabin today while 119 and jewel man are watching the chiefs."

"Yep, from the way Jim described the fellows stalking him."

"So how do we determine that?"

"Going to the police won't help. But it might tell us who else is involved," Rufus said.

"Fine. But you and I know many stalkers and criminals are paid off and only doing what some fancy lawyer or politician is telling them to do."

"Why we're investigators," Rufus said with a smile.

"Yeah. Another reason why I need to get back in church – investigate my own life."

Rufus got silent with that remark: he hadn't gone to church much since he was a child -- when his mother forced him to sit and listen to a preacher talk about hell and brimstone. He hadn't even thought about God since he was on the water one day dredging for clams and a storm came out of nowhere with huge waves and strong winds. Worse, a minute later, a submarine lifted her top and made swells twenty feet high that nearly tipped his boat over. Rufus found himself praying to God for help.

Marcia sat thinking some more as Rufus took a wide swing around a corner and was lost in his own thoughts.

"Be a good idea to see who has represented jewel man in court," Marcia said.

"There is that."

"Is, but not always evident. I'll check on it when we get back."

"And I'll take a ride on the Pocahontas trail."

"See what kind of boots we'll need."

"Or have been there. Good idea. I'll take my boots to kick away the snakes."

"They've probably eaten all of them Rufus. They used to make ornaments out of them."

"James River's got plenty of snakes. I put one on the bow of the boat one day in the heights of my glory."

"Wow. And I thought you were a humble clam dredger."

"Honey. Even a clam dredger needs a little recreation."

When they got back to the office, Marcia had a voice mail on the office phone from Richie who wanted to know if she was busy this weekend.

She thought it over: if she went out with him, it would lead to something else. But she wasn't allowing that, and right now, she was having too much fun investigating.

Besides, there was something about Emma that kept drawing her to know more about the woman, and it wasn't about gold.

She put the phone back in its cradle and decided to call Richie later. It had already been a long day; and now that she and Rufus had a new project with the Indians, she would be occupied.

5.

After she got home and checked for intruders or tricks inside the apartment, she lay on the bed thinking more about Richie.

He is firmly established in his new law firm practice. He litigates product liability and personal injury cases. He has his own condo unit in a prestigious community, and he has money in the bank. But he doesn't have a friend in the world other than me. I can't abandon him, but I'm not ready for a long-term relationship.

She said her prayers to a God who knew best.

And then she called Richie.

"Hi. Got your message."

"Well. What do you think? You available this weekend?"

"Maybe. I got a new project today."

"What happened today?"

"Jim Cloudwaters and Emma Rivers came by and said someone was stalking them."

"Oh? Say who it was?"

"Some fancy men in a black Crown Victoria."

"Probably trying to scare them away from protesting cell phone towers."

"Maybe. I don't know what it's about but it's something that will keep me busy for awhile. What do you have in mind for this weekend?"

"Going out after work Friday night for dinner and whatever else."

"Oh. That sounds nice. Dinner that is."

"Any place special?"

"Surprise me."

"Okay, pick you up after work."

"Fine, Richie. Have a great day tomorrow and we'll talk more then."

Marcia liked to read. She reached over to the bed stand and picked up Eugenia Price's latest novel about two sisters adapting to a strange town. Eugenia would often weave an example of Christian faith in her books.

Marcia yearned for inspiration – after experiencing a troubled childhood with an absent father and three siblings to watch.

But now she felt her destiny and purpose for life was evolving -- glorifying God and witnessing the word. But she definitely needed to get back into church.

She read a couple pages of the book but still thought about Richie.

Maybe he is a distraction. But one date won't hurt.

She rolled back over on the bed and thought about where they might go to dinner -- and how to say goodbye afterwards.

6.

Rufus showed up at work in the morning and told Marcia about his escapade at the Cloudwaters' access road yesterday afternoon.

"The gate was unlocked," he said.

"That would make sense, after they saw me walking towards their car yesterday across the street."

"You scared them off – for awhile anyway."

"Lord, I hope so -- part of my job here."

"You did well. Talk to Captain Tellis?"

"You said "Don't"."

"Well, let's try it. Sometimes when nothing is working – got to make something work."

"Isn't that an old Clint Eastwood saying or something?"

"No. That's what investigator Spenser would say in Robert Parker's novels when nothing was happening."

"You read them too?"

"Do. Why I got this job, ho ho."

Marcia reached for the phone but looked at Rufus momentarily and said, "That theory go for boy and girl relationships too?"

"You bet. Double."

"Might try that out tonight when I see Richie."

"Developing?"

"No, not developing."

Marcia smiled as she looked up the number for the police station in a notebook on her desk.

She got Captain Tellis on the phone and started asking questions about whether the Indians at Jamestown were under surveillance and told him that one of his men was seen in civilian clothes stalking the Cloudwaters.

But Tellis wanted something in return.

"Well, I can tell you the stalker policeman was with another man in a Crown Victoria," Marcia said.

"You get a tag number?"

"I did -- before they screeched off into never-never land."

"Always amazes me how a woman can get a tag number and a man can't."

"It's in the shirt collar, Captain, and respecting the object."

"Yeah. Could be a problem here. There's been another complaint about a policeman stalking someone."

"Well, there you go."

"Internal Affairs handles in-house problems like this. I'll check with them."

"I don't know Captain. That's your job. Our clients were scared to report this to the police."

"Right. And since you got credibility with the department, you're calling as a goodwill mission."

"Exactly. We private investigators and the police need to get along, and I think we're doing a great job."

"We are. Send the tag number via FAX along with the car model and I'll see what I can do. Thank you for calling."

Rufus looked at Marcia and said, "What do you think?"

"I think he knows exactly what is going on."

"The Chief of Police usually does. Probably knows the 119 driver."

"That some kind of federal thing?" Marcia asked.

"Wants everyone to think so, anyway."

"Some kind of international thing?"

"Yeah."

"Well, we can find them. They're only human."

"Most of the time," Rufus said.

7.

As Marcia was driving home after work, gloom and indecisions about her relationship with Richie continued.

But she was looking forward to going out with him and share the day's events and talk about the future.

But Richie wasn't much of a talker, and she always found herself looking for more communication with a man.

He was always understanding and searching for the right thing to say. It was as if he was always trying to figure things out when there wasn't really anything to figure out -- he just needed to respond in faith. He could make conversation much more difficult than it needed to be.

She arrived at her little apartment which was in one of Hampton's low-income complexes.

The sun had disappeared behind the buildings in back of her apartment and it was getting cooler. A little northeast wind was developing and blowing the tops of pine trees.

She entered the apartment and sat down on the couch -- wondering about what to wear for the dinner outing.

She didn't even know where they were going but Richie usually picked a nice place regardless of the cost.

She took a quick shower and decided on black pants with a white collared shirt and a light brown cashmere sweater with buttons --pristine perhaps -- but safe and warm.

She put on a pair of flat black low heels that melded with her pants. She accentuated her shirt with a short tiger eye beaded chain that had a black onyx crucifix at its bottom.

She looked at herself in the mirror and was satisfied -- though the white collar felt stiff. She sprinkled some baby powder on it to reduce the friction around her neck.

She brushed her wavy brown hair letting it fall down over her shoulders and sat down at the dresser.

She glossed her lips and put some musky perfume around her neck.

She got up and grabbed a black evening purse from the closet and went to sit on the couch.

In a few minutes, Richie was at the door looking smart -- with a blue blazer, blue pants, and a white shirt.

She blushed momentarily and bowed her head exiting the doorway -- subtly looking in her purse as if she were looking for something — but unable to keep her mind off Jim, Emma, and Rufus.

Richie could tell something was bothering but he was content to be quiet and let nature have its way, while Marcia wished he'd care more about her issues.

If a man didn't care for her silence or vociferous feelings, what was the use?

They arrived at Morrells Italian restaurant just on the other side of the bridge-tunnel to a packed parking lot.

After entering and sitting down, they were given a bowl of a marinara sauce with fresh herbal cheese breadsticks that could have been dinner by itself.

Marcia ordered a lasagna dish with asparagus tips and grilled mushrooms. Richie would have a meatball dish over rice with a dark sauce laced with basil and sage mixed with stewed tomatoes. A plate of buttered fresh bread was delivered and was set on the table.

The setting was serene, with a view of the bay and the night-lights of the bridge-tunnel reflecting off guardrails and the river.

A group of Navy personnel were in the restaurant with their blue dress uniforms on and were enjoying alcoholic drinks and making noise above the crowd every so often. .

Richie looked at Marcia and said, "So how's the Indian project going?"

"It's off to a roaring start with a couple stalkers of Jim and Emma leaving a parking area in high speed when I walked towards them with an umbrella of all things."

"I think I would have stayed and watched."

"That was the problem. One did and I got his license number before he got away."

Richie felt like he had again put his foot in his mouth.

If he was going to keep her, he had to be more sensitive to her needs, but this always happened when they got together; she would seem offended, and he felt stupid.

Marcia sensed it and said, "Richie, I like Jim and Emma, and I hope to work with them and find out what is happening in their lives. It's something I enjoy."

"Certainly, and I would encourage you to do so."

The waitress brought the food and set each item down on the table very carefully. It was evident she was new to the job and trying to be as careful as possible.

"My second night," she said as she giggled when the meatballs slid a bit to the side of Richie's plate.

"So far, the food is excellent here," Marcia said, trying to relax the young girl's nerves.

"Well, it's fresh and always busy here. Enjoy."

She put the tray back on her hand and walked gingerly to the wait staff area.

Marcia turned her attention to Richie and said, "And the view is pretty. I don't see any freighters on the ocean tonight though."

"Could be there's no one to off-load at port or the Navy has important activity."

"I didn't know that."

"I used to look at the arrival and departure times of the foreign ships in the paper every day. I wanted to be a merchant marine."

"Well, that would have been an interesting occupation."

"Maybe dangerous too -- with ships being hi-jacked and the weather being volatile."

Quietness ensued while they ate and enjoyed their food and drinks: Richie had an imported beer and Marcia drank unsweetened tea.

After dinner, they got in Richie's Toyota and started back across the bridge-tunnel.

"Shall we go somewhere else and park awhile or something?" Richie asked.

"Oh, not tonight, Richie. It's been a long week and I think I'd just like to go home and rest."

"Okay. I understand. I could use the same."

Richie dropped Marcia off at her place and drove to his condo -- looking forward to playing golf with the guys tomorrow.

Always an out, he thought.

8.

After Marcia entered her apartment, she got comfortable in a bathrobe.

She sat thinking about Richie and her future: she felt secure with him but the joy she used to have with him was waning for whatever reason.

She had security -- with her growing faith in Almighty God, and that was really all she needed.

She slept fitfully during the night turning a few times and waking to dreams that did not seem real: they were too confusing to be divine.

In the morning, she washed clothes, cleaned house, and wrote some notes to her brother and sister, who lived on the other side of the Chesapeake Bay.

She baked some cookies and put some fresh fruit in a bowl. Then she went to a dollar store to get a wooden basket and puzzle book for her friend Naomi, who was in the hospital recovering from hepatitis.

When Marcia returned home, she lay down for a while on the bed but the phone rang several times and the answering machine started.

She got up and found that one message was from Rufus -- asking her to call him.

Marcia thought maybe Rufus had got himself into trouble sleuthing because he never called on Saturday.

She dialed his number. "What's up Rufus?"

"I'm going to church tomorrow. You want to go?"

Marcia laughed a little bit and said, "Are you serious?"

"Yeah. Thought maybe I could get some insight on Jim and Ella at their church."

"What about the heavenly word?"

"That too."

"Wow! No place better! Yes, I'll go. What time is service and where at?"

"The Methodist Church on the Parkway to Jamestown on the left at 11:00."

"Cool. Do I need my gun?"

"Not if the preacher is nice."

"Okay. I'll be there!"

And suddenly, Marcia had new joy in her life.

Church, for God's sake. Rufus is going to church! What's got into the man? I mean, I like the both of them, but Rufus is smarter than a Talmudic sage and I like being with him -- investigating!

Marcia immediately went to the bedroom and put away last night's clothing.

She removed a yellow flowered polyester dress from a hanger and laid it on the dresser. She looked in her jewelry box and found an opal necklace, removed a black sweater from the living room closet and draped it over a chair. She found a pair of single strapped black leather flats and set them on the floor in front of the sofa.

She was excited -- some kind of joy she had never experienced. It was a holy joy with her friend and boss, Rufus Stronger, going to church.

9.

Rufus showed up at church in his best dressed attire: of a ruffled double-breasted white shirt, black linen pants, black patent leather spit-shined shoes, and a black suit coat.

No tie for Rufus. It would restrict his movement to get a gun from the back of his trousers.

He had friends here from days of clamming on the James River and docking his boat nearby.

He had also participated in sporting events with these cross-town rivals.

James Mcaultrie and Bernie Regaldo were milling outside the front door before the service started.

Rufus saw to them first before he arrived at the door.

"What's up Rufus? Ain't you high class now with that suit?" James said.

"Comes with the territory."

"Territory must have a lot of money, but we know you ain't here to give your 10%," James said looking at Bernie.

"So what does it cost?"

James and Bernie just smiled.

"Injuns on Pecan Road being stalked," Rufus said.

"Weapons?" said Bernie.

"Something different. Locking Jim and Emma out of road access."

"Don't want them around," said James.

"Reckon why?"

"Something important. Usually money."

"Or valuables," said Rufus.

"Exactly," said Bernie, nodding his head, and looking around suspiciously to see if anyone was stalking Rufus too.

"Like artifacts," Rufus said, getting a feeling for what was happening on the banks of the James.

"They're there. Dragged up a mess one weekend," James said.

"I remember."

Rufus looked around casually at people who were coming to church and parking in the lot. Other people had already parked and were socializing.

"And there's an antiquities guy involved," Rufus said.

"Well, there you go. Sounds like shoreline work or they'd be using a boat," said Bernie.

"May be, but these Indians don't like the metal frame towers neither and they've been opposing them for years."

"Don't no one like those towers and transmission lines up in the air," said Bernie.

"That's true -- been fighting the telephone and electric people from day one," James said.

Rufus nodded his head now wondering if the Indian land conveyed deeded right of ways.

10.

Marcia Lane found the church and parked alongside Rufus' Toyota.

She got out of the car and buttoned her sweater due to the chill coming off the nearby James River. She turned and walked briskly towards the church on a shelled sidewalk to where the three men were talking.

She looked at each them, sizing them up, as they did her.

Tanned skins, weather worn faces, and unkept hair styles figured them to be watermen who worked hard.

Jim took a step back thinking Rufus might know her.

"My God, Rufus. You look splendid!" she said as she approached them.

"Fellows, my co-partner, Marcia Lane."

Both men introduced themselves and became quiet -- figuring Rufus would lead the way with this outgoing pretty woman.

Marcia smiled at them and took a step back to admire the old church brick building with its freshly painted white double doors and tall frontal columns.

"What a beautiful church this is," she said.

"Is. Been here for a hundred years," Rufus said.

Piano music began to play from inside the church and a few people made their way in.

"Shall we all proceed?" said Rufus.

They all went in where most attendees had already found seats.

Rufus led Marcia to an empty space in the fourth pew and sat down to the right of her.

Marcia was not ashamed to be in church; she had been living a rather clean life for the past several years, other than one loving encounter with Richie Granger that went a little too far. And maybe that's why she was here with Rufus Stronger this morning – she wasn't really sure.

She smiled as she sat looking at the choir and rich burgundy curtains behind them.

She calmly lowered her purse to the seat and adjusted her dress; she patted Rufus' hand to show some appreciation and support.

There were times at work when he seemed to antagonize and regret God's dominion over man and earth -- but other times when he seemed faithful to perform good work and mention the Father's name.

She wasn't sure about his faith. She could only encourage him to be a good witness.

Now she was wondering if it wasn't her who needed encouragement -- and direction.

What in the world was I thinking of going to church with my boss! His girlfriend might be here -- but there is no one present.

The inside of the church was beautiful. A vase of purple irises sat on top of a table in front of the speaker's podium, and in the back of the choir, burgundy colored curtains stretched from side to side covering what Marcia thought was a baptismal area. Stained glass windows showing each of the Apostles lined the church sidewalls. The morning sun shone slightly through overtones of blue, red, yellow, and green window panes. The walls were painted a soft white, and the floor was ceramic tile.

The piano music slowed, and Jim Cloudwaters walked in from a side door to stand behind the podium.

Marcia gasped silently and shed a few tears; she did not know Jim was a preacher of the Word.

He welcomed all to church and asked everyone to open their hymnals to sing "Crown Him Lord of All".

Rufus sat solid as a rock as if he was just as comfortable as sitting in his own home.

Marcia looked at him and thought about a big storm with him as helmsman in a boat that was in control. *Lord, Richie would be as giddy as a mouse in a trap.*

After the song ended, Jim spoke of recent church activities and gave updates about sick and missing members.

After another song, by a member, Jim began to preach on righteousness and the right of every individual on earth to be treated with respect and dignity. He said, "God has made each person, male and female in his image, to inhabit the earth and take care of it."

Marcia was beginning to feel comfortable; so she took off her sweater and laid it beside her. She closed the still opened hymnal in her hands and put it back in the rack and opened her Bible to Genesis 1-3.

God would take care of Rufus -- she needed to keep her own life on course right now and stay in the scriptures.

After the sermon, and the plates for offerings were passed, the congregation sang a couple more songs and Jim gave the benediction from the Book of Jude.

Now unto him that is able to keep you from falling, and to present you faultless before the presence of his glory with exceeding joy. To the only wise God, our Savior, be glory and majesty, dominion and power, both now and ever. Amen.

Marcia smiled and glanced at Rufus, who was looking at people exiting the pews. Some were shaking hands, others were talking, and yet others looked as if there was a great ball game on television and they wanted to get home in a hurry.

She dared not interrupt his thinking, knowing he was gauging the situation and trying to figure out who was stalking Jim and Emma.

When he stood up, she quietly gathered her belongings and followed him outside. Rufus waved good-bye to his friends and guided Marcia to the parking lot.

"Shall we take a look at the gate of contention while we're here?" he asked her.

"Why not. If it's close."

"It's two blocks down the road towards the river."

"Let's go. I'll follow you."

When they got to the dirt road and gate, both of them got out of their vehicles and stared at it and the surroundings.

"Don't get too close. Could be some traps here," Rufus said.

Scrub oak and pine trees lined the perimeter of the dirt road, which disappeared into the woods. The river was off to the west a couple of hundred yards, and just south was the old fort at Jamestown, where the first settlers tried to protect themselves from Indian attacks on a small peninsula. It had since succumbed to the weather and strong tidal waters.

Someone had planted white azaleas along the front of the main road, and a ditch headed towards the river.

The gate was 8' long and strap hinged on a plate to a metal post. The gate would reach to a standing metal pole that had a cup for the gate to lie on and be locked with a chain. Today it was open.

Marcia looked for some sign in the surrounding weeds for any evidence of someone who had been in the vicinity while Rufus was carefully taking a walk down the dirt road.

"Hey, wait for me. Hold on, I'm coming with you!"

She thought about the Indians and the long history of them attacking whites.

Had to have been frightening back then, she thought as she chose her steps carefully -- narrowly missing a few mud puddles and stray wood limbs on the ground.

Rufus had stopped. He was looking upwards in the sky, and Marcia, slightly winded, thought maybe he'd seen an eagle, so she looked in that direction.

She couldn't think of what else to say about his upward stare, so she said, "Nice and quiet out here, isn't it?"

Rufus looked distracted and a bit agitated. "Yea, when there's no fighting or arrows flying."

Marcia's thoughts again went back to the 17th Century when the whites and Indians were fighting over land, food, and supplies.

"Well, the settlers were a faithful bunch who had church services," she said trying to be positive.

Rufus chuckled and said, "Yeah, while Chief Powhatan was gathering his braves and planning their resurrection."

They began to walk a few more steps.

"Well, they all got along for awhile. I mean that Chief's daughter married John Smith."

"For a few years," Rufus said, as he turned his head and began to walk back towards the SUV.

"Well, hey! What did you see up there?"

"The metal cage."

"Wow. Indians trap from the trees?"

"No. No. There's a cell phone tower on the other side of the trees."

"Ohhhh. That makes sense. And this group has been fighting them for years. Now someone wants to keep them from sabotaging the tower, so they lock the gate trying to keep them out."

"Probably," Rufus said as he kept his down looking for any clues. "But it could also be a distraction."

"Since egress rights were given for each other to cross each other's lands, someone thinks they can trespass anytime."

"Something like that. But they can't disregard the rights of Indians to be free from foreign interference."

"How so?"

"They are a sovereign nation, plus the court stated that environmental impacts assessments are to be conducted before anything can be constructed on their lands."

"But it was done anyway."

"Was. And watch out for that mud puddle."

"They ought to be taken down."

"Should," Rufus said as he neared his vehicle.

Marcia stopped and looked at him. "What are we going to do?"

"We're going to go home and eat fried chicken. You want some?"

"Lord, that sounds good, but maybe next time. I've already used a bit of your time."

"We're going to find the stalker, look up some land records, and find out what artifacts has to do with this."

"Wow. You got it all planned out."

"Do."

"Hey Rufus. I really enjoyed the service and hope we can go again sometime."

"Yeah, sure, Marcia. Now you have a nice trip home and I'll see you at the office tomorrow."

Marcia almost felt like giving him a hug but this was her boss. She said okay and nodded her head. She got her keys out of her purse and got into her vehicle not thinking about Indians but about the strength and faith of one Rufus Stronger.

11.

Jim Cloudwaters and his two sons, Crow and Blue, sat quietly in their cabin thinking about the cell phone tower nearby -- and the stalker.

Jim's organization, CARES –Citizens Against Remote Electronic Surveillance -- had been fighting against technology that encroached upon their lands for years.

But this stalker seemed to be another issue yet to be figured out.

Jim's daughter, Lilly Mae, was working in the kitchen frying corn pones and making bean bread for lunch.

"The white man and his girl may help us," Jim said.

Crow and Blue sat silently, knowing the old man's wisdom would speak more in due time. As sons, their interruptions would only delay things – empty words at the wrong time.

Jim leaned in his chair towards a pine table that was in front of him with his elbows on his knees. He looked at both of his sons: Crow was a handsome lad with coal black hair which hung straight down. He had clear brown skin. He was slim and tall with narrow shoulders. Blue was the younger at 21 years old and quieter. A little pudgy in the stomach from eating Lilly's pones -- that were usually laced with pork fat -- he could still out rebound anyone in the paint on a basketball court or bull his way through defenders in a stickball game.

Jim spoke up, "We could get an injunction against the company that is planning to build more towers – and request an environmental assessment. But what good would that do, when they own the construction crews and inspectors?"

Blue Jay sat with his head down. He was sharpening a 6" stainless steel knife blade with a whetstone. He angled the blade back and forth over the fine grain stone switching sides while turning its boned handle.

Lilly removed several pones from an iron skillet in the kitchen and wiped up some grease that had fallen on the counter.

"The court favors us from any further aggression," Jim continued. "But what is done, is done. The energy off them towers and transmission lines are bad. The bear, deer, and foxes have left the area. If it wasn't for our protective barriers, the shellfish would probably die. Them towers put out bad energy. All of us have been getting sick with different ailments as a result."

Both boys nodded their heads in agreement.

"Now, this stalker is something else, and I have an idea of what he wants."

Lilly overheard the words, and anger swelled in her body. She felt she had lost a child because of the technology intrusion; the energy had heated up her ovaries and caused too much fluid into the baby.

And their grandmother Emma was showing signs of forgetfulness -- with her hands shaking uncontrollably as the energy disturbed her nerves.

58

After going to high school and nursing college, Lilly knew the white people's ways. She found American history had been fabricated to teach the white man had discovered America.

Worse, false healing methods for the sick were being taught in nursing school.

Who in their right mind would give a sick person a hard pill to swallow knowing the digestive system could not break it down? Worse, people were being injected with germs and told that it would protect them from getting germs.

Blue Jay sheathed the well-honed knife and went to the bedroom to retrieve a battery powered reciprocating saw. He opened the case and took out the charger and battery; he plugged the charger in an electrical outlet.

Crow saw his brother's actions and rose from his chair and walked slowly to the front door. He opened the door and walked outside to look around -- always suspicious of anyone lurking around the area. The birds would tell him, the smells would draw near, and the sounds would direct him.

It was quiet.

He walked to a woodpile and grabbed five loose sticks -- each about 3" in diameter and brought them into the cabin and stuck them in a backpack.

Lilly finished putting corn pones on a plate and took off her apron. She walked over to a closet to retrieve a poster board and markers. She loved to draw and make colorful images -- colors that resembled the sky, grass, trees, and shells.

She brought the items back to the large kitchen table and sat looking at the poster board. The letters would be large and bright: No Trespassing.

It would be a start.

Blue Jay knew what she was doing, and he smiled.

Jim looked at each of his children and was proud. He never had to force any of them to protect the old way to keep the family safe.

There were days that the family fished together with nets -- that made no noise -- unlike boat motors. They had stretched those nets out on the river floor and waited for the tide to bring in a mess of fish. Days when snares and traps could catch wild game to eat -- and in the silence of a morning, a whistled song could attract a bird to be caught and roasted for dinner.

Jim could only hope such days would return.

12.

When Marcia got home, she saw message lights blinking wildly on her answering machine and walked over to check them out.

There were three from Richie and a no-number -- *probably a solicitor,* she thought.

But before she would return Richie's calls, she wanted to think more about her outing with Rufus: she was torn between falling in love with her boss or dating Richie Granger -- a thriving attorney who could give her security for life, at least financially.

That was just it -- choose money or love, she thought.

The day had warmed considerably from the cool morning and dew that had covered the area. The apartment, which had only two windows, one in the living room and one in the bedroom, could get hot -- being made of brick and mortar which absorbed late morning sun-rays.

Marcia shed her sweater and sat down on the couch. Looking out the window to see kids playing in the street and doors from other tenant buildings opening and closing as people were coming and going to church or parks to enjoy the nice weather; she sat in peace.

Spring robins were in the yard pecking for prey on the ground while a squirrel was looking for nuts in the deep brown carpet of leaves under trees in a wooded lot. Daffodils and dandelions were beginning to sprout above the green grass.

Love or money? It was always the choice.

Should she even return the calls? Or wait on the Lord for guidance?

For years, the divine way had been her saving grace.

She had enjoyed the morning with Rufus and not having illicit thoughts about anything!

It was a feeling of being in the right place at church -- around people who could be trusted. And Rufus was a faithful religious man she hadn't known existed until today. Though his work had always showed faith, he never spoke of God.

Quiet confidence was his attribute, and she loved it. She just didn't know where it was going with him. He still liked to play in his off-time. She knew that, but she did too, within reason.

She got up and fixed herself a cup of tea.

She could at least call Riche and tell him the truth -- that she went to get some insight about the Pocahontas trail and fell in love with Rufus. How would that go over!

But it was really none of his business what she did with her time. She wasn't married to him.

The phone call could wait.

*

13.

Marcia awoke to a beautiful Monday morning with clear skies and warmth from spring southwest winds now filling the peninsula with humid air.

Rather than put on her blue uniform for work, she chose a light yellow knit blouse and brown slacks.

A wooden necklace with olive lettered sea shells garnished her neck, and a light coat of lacquer was put on her nails.

She put on some canvas shoes and got her back pack with the.38 caliber pistol in its pocket. A knife and some snacks were still inside the pack.

If Rufus was going to have her walking in the woods around Jamestown, she wanted to be ready, but who knows.

And that's what happened when she got to work.

He told her to load up the boat in the back of the building. She looked at him incredulously as if he had drank too much alcohol.

But no. He was sober and serious.

"Sure Rufus. Where's the gear?"

"At the back of the parking lot in a shed at the corner of the building."

"Cool."

She dared not ask another question because she loved to go boating.

But then she thought of Richie and how he would feel knowing she and Rufus were on a boat together. She had been out with Richie several times in a boat fishing and enjoying the sun.

I have got to get over this. But she could hear the question now, *Investigative work now on the river?*

"Be ready in thirty minutes. I'm going across the street to get us some sandwiches."

"Remember to say Hi to Sherry Linton," Marcia said as she thought about grabbing some different clothes from a tall locker in the office.

Rufus looked at her and said nothing. The last thing he needed was to think about bombshell Sherry at the café; he was disturbed enough with this case and good looking partner Marcia Lane.

After Rufus had left the office, Marcia grabbed a tee-shirt, shorts, and large brimmed hat from a storage locker. She walked gingerly down the steps to the parking lot at the back of the building -- thankful she was not in a stuffy office smelling moldy air from the air conditioning system and having to listen to telephones, copy machines, and the beeping of a smoke alarm which started every time the battery got a little low in courtroom offices. And then there were aggressive lawyers looking for something in documents that was not going to be there.

"Well, I thought Mrs. so and so said that" they'd say.

Marcia would tell them each time: "It's not in the document – the person didn't say it. Comes typed right from the listening machine".

She found the shed at the end of the brick building and stared at it thinking it was an excellent place to change clothes.

She stripped and hung her clothes on a nail and put on her shorts, the over sized tee-shirt, and hat.

The wide hat would look good with her country hair but she knew it would end up in the water with winds blowing across the bow if she wore it on the boat.

She stuffed the hat back in her bag and took out a baseball cap -- pulled the majority of her hair back in a pony tail and stuck it through the opening in back of the hat.

She opened the shed door and smelled a musty odor: the shed must not have been opened for awhile.

There were piles of leaves and yellow stained wind-blown newspapers surrounding the shed and they blew mercilessly as gusts of wind circled the enclave and blew down the debris. Marcia wondered when the area had last been cleaned.

A mouse scooted out from underneath and went around the corner.

She looked through the doorway and saw the life preservers, oars, gas cans, and a couple of fishing poles in a far corner. Getting them one at a time, she put them all in the boat.

The 14" aluminum john boat was on a trailer parked at the other corner of the enclave.

She hadn't been on one in years -- since she had moved from the Bow Creek section of Virginia Beach.

Richie had taken her out boating a couple times on his 20' footer Whaler but she liked being closer to the water and feeling a smaller boat's vibrations against the floor when the boat hit waves. A small john boat would gradually beach itself too after a thrust of the engine with its V shaped-bow.

While standing there beside the boat, she figured they were probably heading to the Jamestown area to get a view of the Powhatan land.

Rufus arrived with a bag of sandwiches and a duffel bag.

He got in his SUV and backed it up to the trailer. After looking in the boat to see if all the supplies were there, he went to the front of trailer and lifted the tongue of it upon the SUV's hitch and put a safety pin in and hooked up a safety chain.

They took off across the James River Bridge to Chuckatuck -- without Rufus saying a word.

Marcia broke the silence. "This sure is interesting detective work Rufus. We taking this thing to the shop or something this morning?"

"Yeah. We're going shopping alright," Rufus said in his usual satirical tone.

It's what made their relationship so unique. They could talk in some kind of encrypted language no one else could understand but they knew exactly what each other was thinking.

The ride over the bridge was nice. There were a few boats on the water and the sea was calm.

"Excuse me, but why are we going on the other side to launch?"

"I like the view better."

Marcia looked at a flag on shore and saw it was as still as the drooping leaves on shore trees.

Then she saw a bird take off from the guardrail and knew the wind to be blowing from the Southwest slightly. But when another gull from the bridge railing lifted itself without turning, she knew there was little wind on the water today other than that being propelled by tidal flow.

They arrived at a tackle and bait shop by the river and Rufus backed the trailer down a boat ramp. Marcia got out of the SUV and had to take off her shoes to get in the water because there was no side ramp or dock to stand on – just an old fashioned concrete boat landing. Fortunately, the sides of the ramp were smooth.

As the sun continued to rise over the water, the wind picked up slightly with a few clouds shadowing the area and coming over the tall pines that lined this west side of the James River.

She admired the bare tree roots along the river's sides -- where storms had taken away sand and left dirt buttresses.

There was only a couple feet of tide drop here, but storms combined with swift running tides during a full moon in the spring or fall made new sand bars and stripped away sands from the banks.

With Marcia hanging onto the rope to keep the boat in the water, Rufus pulled the Toyota up the ramp while yelling to Marcia he had to go inside the tackle shop and pay.

In a few minutes, he came down from the shop smiling and laid a bag in the boat and looked things over including the weather.

Marcia saw his smirk. "You get a call from Sherry or something in there?"

"Better than that – got a free pound of shrimp."

"I should have known."

But before he went anywhere on the water, he bowed his head and said a personal prayer for safety.

Marcia looked on amazement.

After finishing, he said, "Old friends around here."

"Didn't you live somewhere around here?" Marcia said as she stepped inside the boat and straightened things. She moved some items towards the middle where they wouldn't get wet.

"Did a couple miles away," Rufus said as he stepped into the boat with his rubber boots on and sat at the rear ready to pull the starter cord. "See you got your waders on," looking at her bare feet.

"Would have helped if you had given me a warning we were wading today."

Marcia grabbed a flotation cushion to sit on and said, "But that's okay. I'm a water girl and will make do."

She was cute in her brown shorts and a tee-shirt that could surely be seen through if she got it wet. And those couple of hair strands left hanging down in front of her ponytail alongside her ears made her childish looking.

Rufus found himself staring more than he should, but after all, they were a team on a business trip.

They had both attended church yesterday, and in the quietness of the service, he had started thinking about an intimate relationship with her. But he sure didn't want any trouble with her attorney boyfriend Richie Granger, who could make some serious time consuming activities. Besides, Richie often gave him work to do.

And this was a work day; Rufus had a couple of things on his mind about finding out who was stalking the Cloudwaters. And why was a jewel thief involved?

Until he remembered the cache of pearls the Indians had been stockpiling for centuries from oyster and clam beds, he never would have figured it out.

The 15 horsepower motor started on the third pull after the choke was pulled, and Rufus closed the choke and eased the boat further away from the ramp first with a paddle to deeper water just in case there were any obstructions near the ramp.

He dropped its propeller into the water and turned away from the bank at 90 degrees and headed across the river to Jamestown.

14.

They were one-half way to other side of the river but out of the main channel when Rufus throttled the motor down.

"Rufus," Marcia said. "How could you give up a job like clamming on these beautiful waters?"

"Beautiful today but try coming out here on a northeaster when the waves are three foot high on a flood tide during the moon with a loaded boat."

"So you'd maybe only get a couple of days work in during the week?"

"Something like that during the winter. In the summer, I often did a little crabbing to supplement my income. The rest of the time was spent playing pool and cards. That's how I got to know most of the guys at the church we went to yesterday."

"You all played at the church?"

Rufus smiled at Marcia and slowed the boat motor down further as they neared the eastern shore of the river.

"Some kind of denomination," Marcia murmured.

Marcia kept her eyes peeled for any waterborne snakes or obstructions in the water; it wasn't unusual for a tree branch or a part of a pier piling to be floating on the water after a storm.

The boat rocked slowly from the waves it had just created as they neared the eastern bank at Jamestown.

Rufus pointed north along the shore. "Used to be an oyster reef right there."

"Probably why the colonists pitched their tent here -- to have something to eat."

"Had to be. There's another reef farther upstream."

"Imagine Rufus. Landing in a foreign country with few supplies and not knowing where to get some food to eat would be a death warrant."

"Especially being the city dwellers they were and not being sea worthy. Not difficult for us poor seaside folk to hunt and fish, but they didn't know how to hunt for game, fish, or earthly goods."

"Evidently, with them all dying that first year."

Rufus dropped the anchor over the side, and the boat drifted until its chain became tight – about twenty yards offshore.

Rufus sat still – looking on shore for any sign of movement or disturbance in the trees – which would tell him if anyone was in the woods.

The boat sat silent, with an occasional wave lapping its side on the starboard side. Marsh grass from the shore returned ripples of water back to the boat. A few minnows swam by as a large blue heron stood silently in the weeds looking for food.

Jim Cloudwaters' land spread thirty acres along the river and 800 feet inland which put him above the flood line yet provided equity to two small tributaries of the James River that Rufus thought were good for raising and harvesting Virginia oysters -- some of which could develop shiny pearls in brackish water.

The Indians never advertised their products but Rufus knew something heavy was in their boats the way they were low in the water from his days of clamming.

Gathering oysters in the James had been a long time tradition for the Indians until the English had come and ravaged the oyster beds and failed to replenish them.

When the English built factories upstream after a swarm of new settlers had arrived, pollutants entered the James, and centuries later, the James would have to be closed for years because of the contamination.

Marcia had her phone camera out taking a few pictures of the shoreline.

"Marcia. Hand me that rake from under the bow please."

Marcia looked under the boat's metal bow and grabbed the rake and gave it to Rufus.

"Be hard to start a garden out here," she said.

"Ain't hard to clam though," Rufus said as he extended the rake over the side of the boat and pulled it up quickly. On its tines were several clam shells.

"Got some shrimp from the tackle shop but with this running tide, let's try these shells."

He opened a shell and a gluey textured muscle oozed onto his hand. He set it on the seat.

Marcia looked on with interest figuring Rufus might add these clams to the sandwiches he had bought, but he lifted one of the fishing poles and baited a hook and handed it to Marcia.

"I've never used clam for bait," she said.

"Catch red drum with these babies."

Marcia's eyes lit up and she cast the rig back towards the channel in the running tide.

The tide was right, and a drum hit softly within a minute, but she yanked too quickly and missed it.

"Play with him a while. It's like a flounder, give it back to him a little, and then come in with it easy."

She put a new clam on the hook and cast it back in the same spot, felt the pole tug ever so softly and gave it some slack, and then came in firmer with it.

She had the fish on -- a two-pounder that gave her a fight until she landed it into the boat.

"Wow. That was fun. I've never fished for these before."

"They'll also band around grass beds looking for food."

"Shall we keep it?"

"Naw. We ain't got no ice."

"Probably be alright till we get home."

"Would, but maybe next time."

She unhooked the fish and returned it to the water. "That was nice!"

"Was," Rufus said. "Let's take a little ride along the shore and see if we can find anything out of the ordinary."

"This whole day has been out of the ordinary."

Marcia dipped her hands into the water to clean them of fish residue and wiped them dry on a towel.

"Could be worse," Rufus said.

"Lord, I hope so."

Marcia felt herself getting excited and pulled her knees toward her arms while looking at the open waters towards the bay and wondering about her love life.

She shook her head slightly to get the hair out of her eyes and smiled with the wind hitting her face and hair strands flying to the side.

15.

"Let's traverse the shoreline awhile and look for anything suspicious like tree cuttings, vehicle tracks, or strange boats. You get a picture of that boat off the starboard side? It's been there awhile," Rufus said.

"Not a close-up. Give me the bigger camera and I'll see if I can get a number off its side."

Rufus reached in the duffel bag and retrieved a 10x zoom digital camera and handed it to Marcia.

"Take pictures of the shoreline too in case we miss something."

After slowly traveling a mile up the river, Rufus stopped and anchored near a grass bed and cast out a fishing line with some clam on it and sat still.

Marcia was working on taking manual pictures with the camera and opening the f-stop to allow more light into the sensor to get a better picture of the shady side of an anchored boat at the edge of the channel.

Rufus caught nothing on the clam, so he loaded up the two hooks with some of the shrimp and threw the rig back towards the channel.

That failing, he put some artificial bloodworms on the rig and caught a few spot fish. He threw each of them back in the water while looking at Marcia putting the camera back in its case.

"That's good," Rufus said. "How about those sandwiches now?"

"Sounds good. At the local picnic shelter or right here?"

"At the shelter."

Marcia had no idea where the shelter might be but she knew Rufus would.

Rufus pulled anchor and started the motor and angled the boat to some high ground on the eastern bank where there were some steps and rails leading up out of the water and into a yard and house.

"Ain't this cool?" Marcia said as she looked over the property.

"Old homestead, probably tied up in estate proceedings. Been vacant for years."

"Well, it is a great looking place," she said with wide eyes and erect shoulders. There are three stories with white columns in its rear. Tall windows are on the first floor. And look at the iron fence, probably around a garden. Let's go check it out! An overgrown grape vine is taking down that trellis."

Rufus brought the boat close to the steps while Marcia took a rope leading from a cleat and clove hitched it to a rail post.

She got out first not even looking at Rufus but looking at the plantation home before her.

Rufus had turned the motor off but waited until the boat stopped rocking to step ashore after Marcia's departure had sent the bow skyward. He gathered the duffel bag, which had the sandwiches from Rosie's and various supplies in it. One was a tarp he often used as a poncho – but today, it would be a ground cover to sit on.

"Lord, wouldn't you like to live here?" Marcia exclaimed out loud as she walked in wonderment looking over the farm area that sat along the water's edge.

"Maybe. Maybe not," Rufus yelled back, as he unfolded the tarp. "Taxes could be high and water could be a problem."

"But not Indians."

Rufus just smiled, always admiring Marcia's sense of humor.

"Reckon not."

Rufus spread out the tarp on the sloped piece of ground and put the sandwich bag down.

Marcia turned and came back to sit on the tarp and enjoy the view of the river.

"After they both ate, Rufus laid out on the tarp and began to close his eyes. The sun was shining intermittently and there was a cool breeze coming off the water.

Marcia was still excited from looking at the house, and she stared at the water while sitting erect. She was thinking about life: Richie, Rufus, and God Almighty.

"Deep in thought?" Rufus said. "Take a break girl. Relax. We still got to get back across the river and unload."

"Well, the turkey sandwich with all the trimmings has me in another world. It was very good but I can't see Sherry making it for me."

"She thought they were both for me."

Marcia smiled and smiled, "Must have."

She began to relax – turning over and putting her elbows on the tarp and stretching her legs out.

"Okay, but just for a few minutes. I want to go exploring."

Rufus just shook his head and closed his eyes.

Marcia took a deep breath and lay down with her head on her hands to the side thanking God for experiencing something her ancestors had probably done hundreds of years ago in this same place.

Peace and quiet along the riverbanks of the James.

But the ruffling of leaves nearby disturbed the sanctity of her thoughts and being alone with Rufus along the James River on a nice summer day.

16.

She lifted her head and looked over to a patch of brush where a deer was escaping from the brush and running towards the house.

Wonder what spooked her?

Looking at the perimeter of the brush area, she saw nothing but a vulture circling the sky overhead and drifting with the air currents.

Rufus was near asleep, with his belly moving slowly up and down and a grunting from his nostrils.

Marcia thought about reaching over and putting her hand on his heart to feel the rhythm of his being, but her inner feelings thought it could lead something too intimate.

Marcia's Japanese boyfriend years ago had taught her about a man's nature by listening to and feeling his heart.

She yearned to get closer and breathe with him -- inhaling and exhaling to the soft beat of a man who God had created to do good works.

A gust of wind against her hair brought her back to reality. She looked to the river and saw a couple of boats and some sea gulls following a shrimp boat.

She shook herself free of lustful thoughts -- rubbed her eyes and forehead to make sure she was still on the tarp.

What in the world was I thinking about? Rufus is my boss, not my lover.

Marcia thought about the deer going to the front of the house, and that's what she really wanted to see – the house.

She shook her head again and slowly got up off the tarp and straightened herself up.

Rufus could wait, and besides, he needed rest to get her back across the river.

She drew her hair back and looked around for anyone near the house.

The rumbling of a motor towards the front of the house caught her attention; so she picked up the camera at the end of the tarp and walked over to the grape vine arbor for some protection. Surrounding the arbor was a garden of overgrown sage, thyme, and lavender plants.

As the roar of the engine slowly faded away, she saw and smelled a magnolia tree that was bursting out with large white flowers on the near side of the house and sending a sweet aroma throughout the yard. Two pomegranate bushes were up against the side of the house in the shade, and Marcia saw several ripe pomegranates. She picked a couple and put them in the camera bag.

Off the back patio walkway was a door leading to a room in the basement, which she thought to have been the kitchen and where fires were stoked.

A brick walkway went to the side and front of the house. A couple of yards off to the side was a corral and pen —she figured for animals – though many animals such as hogs would have been free to roam the woods for food. That was another item of discontent for the Indians --who did want their crops ravaged by the white's animals.

The pen was dilapidated with rotten logs upon each other. An overhang angled towards the sky with its corner posts was the only supports standing.

She followed the walkway around.

The windows of the house looked of lead glass – swirled with darkness within their iron frames. She looked into one window and saw stairs leading up to a second floor -- with cob webs dropping from the rails.

Wood cornice work showed kings and horses at the top of the walls. Marcia thought the house to be early 18th century.

Whoever owned and built it must have had lots of money because the house was made of brick and mortar. The wood work was not done by ordinary carpenters: there were mortise and tenon joints at corners, carved wood decorations, and smooth surfaces on the wood.

There were brick fireplace chimneys on each side of the house that went upwards of the roof. Asphalt shingles now covered the roof. One sidewall had been burned, as smoke stains covered its exterior wall. Marcia saw several buckets nearby and wondered if they were used for putting out fires.

Yankees could have set the fires during the war, she thought.

Marcia walked to the front of the house and saw an iron railed balcony on its second floor.

Two small paved roads led out from the house.

There were plum and myrtle trees surrounding the area. She walked over to the plum tree and picked several -- all the time thinking about how she would love to live at this place.

She took a few pictures and hurried back to see if Rufus was awake, while a plane flew overhead real low at the same time.

She ignored it and saw Rufus sitting up drinking something.

She walked over proudly and said, "Hey. Look what I got," showing off the pomegranates and plums.

Rufus turned his head to see Marcia with the purple and red fruits in her hands.

"Won't beat this wine cooler I brought," he said gruffly while reaching into an insulated bag for ice.

"You devil. You didn't say anything about that."

"Didn't know if you would approve."

"Will if you give me some."

Rufus poured her a tin cup of Moscato wine and gave it to her.

She lifted it up as a signature: "To the beauty of the James and good friends."

Rufus clashed his cup and said "Amen."

Marcia finished her cup in a few swallows and felt the warmth hit her face.

"That was good. How about one more?"

"Only if you don't get mushy on me."

Marsha giggled. "Are we still on duty?"

She took another cupful and sat down beside him and looked up at his broad face and black hair and thought about what a wonderful boss he was, and now he was becoming something else.

She shook her head a little. "I think that was enough for me. Shall we get going?"

"I can't drink and drive."

"I'll drive Rufus." Where's the boat?"

"I'll drive. You carry the luggage and load up."

Rufus got up and stretched his legs and walked to the edge of the river, thinking about Marcia, the Indians, clamming, and the stalker. All the days he had spent on the river clamming were now gone. This was a new life being a detective, but it was a joyful one and more lucrative financially than weighing baskets of clams and oysters only to be told the price had fallen.

After the tarp was put back in the duffel bag, they descended the concrete steps and carefully got back in the boat.

Rufus pulled the cord and the motor came alive spitting out smoke and vibrating turbulence through the water.

Clouds were becoming thicker in the sky as they usually do in the late afternoons on summer days. The wind picked up but the tide was ebbing, which would make their trip easier as Rufus would angle the boat westward across the river to the boat ramp.

Marcia was laid back and lifted her shirt up partly to tan her belly area. She rolled up her shorts.

Rufus just smiled as he looked at her and was glad to have a partner that was smart, pretty, and funny -- even if she couldn't hold her alcohol.

She smiled as she ate some crackers and wondered if they could do this again sometime.

Rufus pulled the boat up to the ramp and he threw a line to Marcia who was sitting on the middle partition smiling and stone-faced. He got out and went to get the Toyota.

They trailered the boat and went back to the office in Newport News and unloaded all the gear.

They looked at each other beside the Toyota for a minute with Marcia was still smiling yet flushed from the alcohol.

"That was fun Rufus. I hope we check the shoreline out again one day," as sweat beaded on her forehead and straggly hair covered her half-closed eyes.

"We will. Look, tomorrow check the county records about the Indian land and who technically owns it; look into who owned that boat on the river, and find out more about that jewel thief. I'm taking the day off and see if I can make sense out of this case. When I can't figure things out, I usually do nothing."

"That sounds like fun too. Can I come?"

"Need me, give me a buzz. Oh, might as well talk to Tellis and find out whatever."

"Well I hope you have a happy day," Marcia said as she was still giggly from having the wine, boat, and car ride. She looked at him seductively and moved towards him.

He gave her a little hug and said, "And put some clothes on!"

"Well, it was hot on that boat," Marcia said as she backed off and untied the loop knot from her t-shirt and un-cuffed her shorts.

When Marcia got home, she took a quick shower and immediately lay down to say her prayers and thank God for the nice day.

After a few minutes, she fell asleep.

17.

Jim Cloudwaters sat in the living room of his cabin thinking about all the ways the white man had encroached upon his property.

The shore had been dredged of prized shellfish, trees had been cut down for trails, the earth had been dug up for wires, and high metal towers had been placed in prime hunting areas.

At times, he sat and cried.

The tears had also showed on Emma's face.

They would walk through the woods and look for animals that weren't there any more; the nuts from trees looked waterlogged; and the fish from the river would have orange oxide bellies.

And many of their people had died from new diseases and oppression.

The towers coming down could wait, but this stalker had to go. He could be trying to steal something Jim and his fathers had worked on for hundreds of years.

The pearls foretold the weather, repelled evil spirits, brought good fortune to the wearer, and absorbed the worst of poisons in the native waters – at least until the whites brought foreign chemicals to the area.

Crow had an idea: he went outside and gathered some stakes for marking off-limit areas. Then he went to the shed in back of the cabin and retrieved three spring loaded bear traps – the kind that would snap shut on any foot.

He brought the items back to the house, and Jim just smiled.

"That ought to do it. Lilly, you say that gate is locked again?"

"Yes, Daddy. And someone started clearing a path around it."

"Okay. Crow and Blue. Let's put up "No Trespassing" signs at the gate, cut the lock again, and put a couple traps right at the latch area. Cover the traps with a few weeds after you bury them about four inches in the ground to make them level with the soil. Lilly, draw us up some signs that say "Danger" and we'll put them in front of the gate, along with the words "Not liable for injury". As usual, check out the troughs and make sure the Oyster Catcher bird is not having dinner in the pools. Check the dam gates and get rid of any toad fish or oyster drills you see."

The three men grabbed their tools and signs and walked three hundred yards down the road to the gate.

Crow leveled the ground with a flat rock in several spots and laid the traps down. He swung each of the trap's metal teeth back to a pin – that when disturbed – would release the teeth to clamp down on a ridged bar that would trap whatever set if off.

Crow also took a couple of 2 x 4 boards and hammered 16 penny nails through them with the sharp points exposed. He laid a few boards alongside the dirt road where if anyone walked, they were sure to get spiked.

The local Indians knew of such defensive measures and would not wander off the road.

Blue hammered some posts in the ground and screwed signs to them. He took out his saw from a bag and cut the lock with a metal blade and discarded the lock into the woods.

Jim nodded at both of them; he looked across the street to see if anyone had been watching, and they began the walk back home.

Jim was satisfied he'd done all he could do to protect his investment of the land and gemstones.

18.

Marcia woke up in the morning with new feelings about her boss Rufus Stronger.

Surely this will pass. I'm on a path to get my investigator's license – not a marriage certificate.

She arrived at the office promptly at 9:00 and checked the phone for messages.

Hearing none, she turned on the computer to check deed records of the Cloudwaters' land along the James River.

The 30 acres was in his name but there were multiple right-of-ways that had been assigned by power of attorneys who represented electric, telephone, and gas companies.

A quit claim deed went back to 1752 to a Bartholomew Plover.

Somewhere or someone had recognized this was Indian Land as there was a document that stated the Bureau of Reclamation had audited one land transfer with notice – but there was no summary action.

Marcia looked at the map parcel, tax documents, and a survey, which showed the access road and utility structures right where they were located. But there was no approval by the Cloudwaters for any of the easements.

She wanted to see more and planned to go to the county courthouse to get a better look at the documents.

She printed off a map of the property and adjoining properties, whose owners could be causing trouble for the Indians. She could get a better map at the mapping office if there was a survey done.

She also researched who owned the house further up the river where she and Rufus had their picnic lunch.

She loved that place, with its quiet view of the river and surrounding fruit trees.

It was certainly big enough at three stories but all those fireplace flues running along the side of house would allow unnecessary wind drafts.

There were a multitude of parcels and houses along the river, but she couldn't identify the address of the house.

Nice to dream about it.

She then delved into the records of one Reginald Fuzman, supposed jewel thief according to Baily -- the crime boss on Peninsula's east side.

When she had gathered enough of Fuzman's personal information from a recent felony conviction from the criminal court, she entered his name into the state's criminal database and saw there were 11 charges over a decade.

Marcia looked at the attorneys involved and figured some may be involved in this scheme to harass the Indians for whatever purpose.

Fuzman had graduated from petty thefts in retail establishments to car stealing and robbing liquidators of estates and their valuables.

Marcia printed off the report and sat it down on the desk and walked over to the window to look at the traffic. Rufus always walked to the window when he was stumped about something.

Taking a break is good, Marcia thought as she looked down the street and wondered if Rufus was sitting in the café flirting with Sherry Linton; which reminded her, she should call Richie and talk to him.

He had no one but her -- probably because of his churlish ways, but what trial lawyer wasn't a grudge – part of the job, she thought.

She gathered up the notes about the Indian land and locked up the office and drove to the county land deeds office.

It was no surprise to see her car's windshield smeared with soap and a group of workers blocking the parking lot exit while they were working on the sidewalk.

She immediately waved for them to move, and they did slowly move a wood barrier out of the way.

19.

Rufus woke up and fixed himself a cup of coffee and a sandwich and sat down to think about the Indians, Marcia, and Richie, whom he knew was crazy about Marcia.

But what did he care about a full-time relationship? He was having fun as it was, and, if something more happened, it just would. Besides, Sherry Linton across the street in the café was starting to talk more and think less – which he despised. The blueberry pie wasn't that good to keep him around.

He finished but a bite of his sandwich and walked outside the bungalow to look for a cat that had been hanging around for a week. He heard the meowing before he saw her, and he threw the bread in front of her where she quickly attacked it.

He came back inside and sat drinking the rest of his coffee.

Today was going to be play day: he had been working had for several weeks, surveying a cheating husband, watching for thieves at a housing project, and finishing up financial reports at the office.

Besides, Marcia was at the office, and she could handle anything that came up.

He put the empty coffee cup in the sink and put on a pair of shorts, a solid blue polyester knit short-sleeve open collared shirt, and some boat shoes. He always shot better pool in boat shoes because he felt more balanced.

He grabbed his cue stick wood case from the closet -- checked to see that the tip pricker, shaper, and scratch pad for wiping the stick down occasionally were there. The jump and break cue shafts were also there.

His playing cue stick had a 13mm shaft for easy stroking. He had made this case personally from a 2 x 4 piece of wood and clamshell baseboard for the hinged top.

Locking the apartment door and getting in the Toyota, he took off to Harleigh's Pool Room in Suffolk where he knew he would find some answers about what was happening with the Indians. The players were street savvy.

The pool room was an old hangout where a few old friends were always playing pool in mid-afternoon.

He arrived at 12:00.

The darkened windows, wooden log walls, and a carpeted floor that had four 9' Brunswick pool tables was like home to Rufus – since he grew up a few miles away.

Harleigh Jones was where he usually was: sitting behind a small counter looking over his room.

"Roof," he yelled out.

"Hey man. Where is everybody?"

"They'll be here. What you doing here on a work day?"

"Eh. You know how it is. A man's got to take a break some time."

"Speaking of a break. Rack them up and I'll play you a game. Two bucks on the five ball and two on the nine."

Rufus knew Harleigh was always up for a nine-ball game with money on it.

Harleigh grabbed a pool stick and put a rack on the table. He filled the rack with nine balls from the pockets.

After tightening the balls within a triangle wooden rack, he inserted the rack into a slot at the end of the table.

Rufus made a couple of balls on the break sinking the 2 and 4 balls but got stymied on a 1 ball shot at the far end of the table.

Harleigh finished pocketing the balls with a combination 8-9 shot that won the game. Harleigh walked behind the table and moved four plastic pieces on a string line marker above the table that tallied up the money count.

A couple of other players came in and Rufus settled his debt to Harleigh, and they all began a ring game.

Joel Nantone was there.

"What's going with you Rufus? You never come here on a weekday anymore. Work slowed?"

"Got a problem over on the other shore I can't figure out. Or I should say the Indians got a problem."

"And one for you to solve," Joel said as he lined up a shot and bent down bridging his left hand for the cue stick.

"Something like that," Rufus said as he let Joel shoot before talking too much.

Joel said, "Indians always got problems. Had since they've been here."

"Yea. I've always felt a little sorry for them."

"But not everyone does."

"No. It's a cruel world."

"Especially when it comes to land and money."

"Powhatan leader over there has someone stalking him."

"Not a love quarrel?"

"No. The big boys are involved and a jewel thief."

"Probably the oysters."

Rufus thought about that for a second and it finally dawned on him about what was going on.

"My daughter went on a few dates with an Indian boy over on the far shore, and one day, he gave her a beautiful pearl necklace for her birthday – stones I had never seen before."

Rufus stood motionless with his pool stick butt resting on the floor and listening to Joel. Joel was on a run of five balls and shooting the 6 ball.

"Prettiest rocks I've ever seen, and I mean red pearls, opal pearls, and white pearls with fire-like streaks in them."

Joel was part Indian himself – originating from the Tuscarora Nation just south of Virginia – a group the colonists could not colonize.

"So they're harvesting oysters and maybe clams with special fertilization techniques?"

"May be injecting the nacre with special minerals and chemicals to produce those pearls," Joel said.

"My guess. And have been for years."

There was a few moments of silence as Joel continued to make balls while a couple other players sat on nearby bar stools with their sticks leaning against the wall. They were in no hurry to shoot. Besides, a lot could be learned in a pool room listening to Joel and Rufus.

Joel finished by banking the nine-ball off a side rail into a corner pocket.

He looked up and said, "The Indians know physics and chemicals – they had to -- to survive."

106

Rufus just nodded his head and went to the end of the table to rack up the balls.

Any time something good comes out of something ugly, the whites want to try and figure out why, Rufus thought.

"Don't got enough sense to clean up their own lives with Mother Nature to see it," Rufus said.

Joes knew what he was talking about "Right. Like Jesus. Only the poor and humble see to produce something magnificent."

"Amen."

The four played a couple more ring games.

When Rufus was even money, he said good-bye and went home.

He had found what he was looking for, and now he knew why the Indians were being harassed.

Maybe he could put a stumbling block in the stalker's path, unless Jim Cloudwaters had already done so.

20.

Marcia arrived at the county offices complex just after noon.

The red brick building that housed the deed records was situated behind a larger building according to a sign that was at the sidewalk entrance.

She walked towards the office and admired the white crepe myrtle trees along the walk.

She scurried by a couple who were arguing outside the door to the lands records building. No doubt it was probably over land, Marcia thought.

She saw the sign for the deeds office and opened the door and told the lady at the receptionist's desk that she wanted to search the database of some property at Jamestown.

"You got some location of the land or the parcel number?" the lady asked.

Marcia retrieved the land's description from a piece of paper in her side pocket and gave it to the woman.

She waited while the woman looked on her computer.

The woman wrote down some Book and Page numbers of the deed and asked Marcia if she had experience looking up deeds.

"Yes, I was a court clerk for some time in the Hampton area."

Marcia was directed to an adjacent room that contained hundreds of books lining shelves and were stored in open faced cabinets.

The sight turned her mind back to when she researched land ownership for a litigant who was claiming to own something she didn't: it was in her husband's name and bought before the marriage.

Marcia quickly found the right book and turned to the page number and saw the original deed to the property.

The land had been deeded to the Cloudwaters in 1758.

She took the Book to the copy area and had the attendant make her two copies.

She also found right of way documents that had been inserted between the pages but there were no documents with the Cloudwaters' signatures for approval.

After paying the clerk, Marcia took the copies and quickly walked out the door thinking she might have found something that validated the Cloudwaters position about owning the land free and clear of foreign interference.

She stopped by the mapping office and got a large map of the survey of the property – that was dated in 1950.

Then she went straight home with the documents and put them under her pillow.

She had had enough experience with criminals to know they would go to any length to stop a person from investigating their crimes.

She would sleep with the documents behind the locked doors of the bedroom.

21.

Rufus showed up the next morning at the office with a smile on his face.

"Find you a new girl friend yesterday?" Marcia said as she kept her head bowed over the land documents.

Rufus said nothing but went to a closet to retrieve some files from a cabinet.

He figured Sherry Linton might have called wondering where he was, and he didn't need drama this morning.

"May have a lead now," he said.

"Yeah, Well, I got one too."

Rufus looked over from his desk area and said, "Oh. What did you come up with?"

"Filed right of ways and egresses."

"No agreement by the Cloudwaters to give right of ways?"

"None that I could see. And I checked the deed book for conveyances, right of ways, adjoining property issues, and maps."

"You get a copy of the land map?"

"Certainly."

"Let me see it."

Marcia passed a reduced version of the original map to him.

"There are utility lines drawn on here, and the towers," Rufus said, as he looked it over.

"Don't mean the family agreed to it."

"No. Many companies operate under an eminent domain statue that gives them some right to do what they want – if it serves public use."

"But they can't make a profit out of it."

"You know. You are right. Reckon who the companies are?"

"Thought you would never ask," Marcia said. "There's a Manson's Tower Construction, Dominion Power easement grant, and a Chesapeake Telephone Company right of way. Nothing signed by the Cloudwaters."

"Indians would not have agreed to the construction of anything on their lands by the whites."

"No. I wouldn't either if it was my land along the James River."

"May need Richie to look over this. Hey. You look up the status of that mansion we were at?"

"Did. But I couldn't find the address. There's lot of such places around there."

A silence ensued over the office except for the water cooler looking for air and making bubbles.

"Excuse me boss but you never answered my question about why you came in the door looking like you struck gold."

"Well, I think I have. Just got to check out a couple more items and ask a few questions. The Cloudwaters aren't poor Indians. And they like oysters."

22.

At Rufus' request, Jim and his mother showed up the next day at the office to talk more about their land and business.

After polite greetings, and the two of them sat down, Rufus said, "Well, what is there that would make these perpetrators want your land so bad?"

Jim looked at his mother hesitantly – as if seeking permission to tell the truth.

Emma just bowed her head.

Jim knew he needed help on this issue and he would have to trust Marcia and Rufus.

"Pearls," he said.

"Well. Pearls are everywhere," Rufus said.

"Not these pearls."

Marcia looked the other way thinking about pearls: black, white, and yellow ones.

Rufus waited for Jim to speak.

"We've mutated them with a distinct ingredient to integrate the nacre that hardens over time to produce a non-corroding luster."

"Oh," Rufus said, as he imagined the process of pearl farming and the conditions needed to produce genuine pearls.

"Is that why some of my clam areas were empty every couple years."

"Maybe. We were there first."

"And you use clams as the hitching agent."

"Maybe that too. What do you all say? Proprietary secret. But a host of shellfish could be used."

"And you got a cache of these sitting there."

Jim looked straight ahead with a smirk on his face while Emma started twirling a large pendant on her necklace.

"Got a few eggs too."

Marcia and Rufus looked at each other.

It took both of them a minute to think about the connection and Rufus did not want to know anything else; he determined the Indians were specializing in fertilizing oysters to produce quality pearls.

"And so this stalker is not only after your pearls but the recipe."

"Got that right. We have found our windows suddenly unlocked – and strange footprints around the cabin."

"Could sue him for trespassing," Rufus said.

"Or take a knife to his throat."

"There is that, but that would do jail time."

"Why I hired you and angel here."

"It is, isn't it?

The room was quiet for awhile until a car door slammed down on the street below and a couple could be heard talking out loud.

Clouds were moving quickly across the blue sky and a heat pump compressor could be heard rumbling on top of a building.

Rufus spoke up, "Well. The stalker ain't going to quit, and there is probably someone bigger behind this operation. Thanks for coming by Jim. We'll be in touch sometime next week and tell you what we've found out."

With that, Jim and Emma walked out the door and smiled.

"Let's go across the street and get a hot dog," he said to Emma. "Hear Rufus has a girlfriend over there."

"He doesn't have to travel that far."

"You think he's got a hankerin for blondie?"

"That and more."

23.

"Looks like we may have to keep the dirt road under surveillance," Rufus said to Marcia after Jim and Emma had closed the door and walked down the stairs.

Marcia waited until she knew the Cloudwaters had closed the door downstairs before responding. If Indians could hear through the woods a mile away, they could surely hear downstairs.

"And then what do we do? Now that we know the Indians got a stash of pearls and recipes no one in the world has?"

"Put the perpetrators in jail?"

"Oh that will surely work with Tellis in charge and his loonies helping the stalker. Be good if they'd do their job."

"But they won't."

The phone rang and Marcia and Rufus looked at each other for a second, when Rufus nodded for her to pick it up.

"Stronger's Investigative Service."

"Well hello Marcia Lane. How are you today?"

"Chief. I know you did not call to discuss the weather or check on my health. You want to speak to Rufus?"

Tellis ignored the question -- thinking he could get better information from Marcia; so he got right to it. "Had a little problem in Indian Country last night."

"No, certainly not, not with all the treaties that have been signed."

"A man got caught in a trap on a public access road to the Cloudwaters."

"Public for whom? Utility companies and law enforcement?"

"Well, there is that, but the man had to receive doctor's attention."

"Could have been worse I suppose. What was the man doing there?"

"Well, that is a good question and I intend to ask that."

"Sounds like trespassing to me."

Rufus looked on and urged Marcia to keep talking and find out more.

The water cooling compressor turned on and a fly kept buzzing the office looking for a way out.

"Plat's a matter of disputation Chief from my research."

"You do get around, don't you?"

"I like to stay informed in this work. So what is a fellow policeman rambling around with a jewel thief and stalking the Cloudwaters?"

"There could be that, and we are looking into it."

"I'll warn the landowners about trapping in unauthorized areas but the records clearly shows that road is Indian property."

"Hadn't thought of that. May have to disclaim jurisdiction over this issue."

"Sounds good Chief. Anything else you would like to discuss?"

"No, no. You all stop by and see me sometime."

"Rufus doesn't care for your brand of coffee."

Rufus just bowed his head and shook it.

"Might can change that too."

Marcia hung up the phone

"Indians like to hunt," Rufus said.

Marcia chuckled and said, "Humans or animals. Reckon what kind of trap that was?"

"Probably a ground metal spring loaded clamp trap."

"The best kind. They'll be back. You want first or second watch?"

"Let's find out the family's schedule. See when they're gone. The stalkers are most likely to enter the area then."

"Yeah. Park a good ways away though. Can't call Jim about this."

"No. The perpetrators would know."

"So, we do it discreetly. Like right on Sunday morning when they know Jim and family are at church. I get paid extra for Sunday work?"

"If you're good."

24.

Reginald Fuzman had been enamored with jewels since he was a kid finding garnets, rubies, and an occasional emerald stone near his childhood home in Franklin N.C.

There was also an old mine shaft in a nearby mountain where quartz veins ran along the sides. If a man chipped away enough of the outer layers, gold specks could be found.

He would take some of the flecks home and admire them.

As he grew up, he saw the money that could be made from people buying gemstones – and fake gemstones. So he got a job working the mines.

A landscaper friend would haul out dirt out from a native mine but Reggie would sift for rubies and garnets and put a few of the smaller stones back in the dirt. The load would be hauled to a site where tourists would buy a screen for ten dollars in search of small gems in a sleuth of channeled water.

Reginald took part in this money making scheme by selling buckets and screens and making sure they were filled with low quality gem stones.

However, it was embarrassing one day when a lady bought a bucket and found several pieces of trash in it along with some hosiery fabric.

Word got around this mine was fake and she had gotten the shaft.

Today, he was re-thinking his motives for acquiring high quality gemstones in the form of pearls he had heard the Indians were making at the end of an estuary.

His leg was painful sore from stepping in that trap and his hand hurt from separating the trap's teeth. In a hurry to leave, he had scraped his arm on a briar bush that left prongs in his skin.

If a leather boot had not been on his foot, he surely would have suffered a more fatal injury than just a big bruise and swelling above his ankle. The doctor he visited was no help by giving him pills.

"That thing could have killed me!" he said over the phone to his partner and a part-time policeman, Paul Gunther.

"Well, watch where you're going!"

"This ain't going to work. Can't keep locking the gate and expecting the Indians to up and leave. They've cut the lock three times now, and what about angel face and her boyfriend watching us?" Reggie said to Paul.

"Don't worry, Mr. Balogne says it's all under control. If you want to stay out of jail for those previous break-ins, you better find a way to get in that building and get those gems."

"It's concrete, right?"

"No. It's a wood cabin -- just down the path a few hundred yards past the dammed up areas in the middle of a slew of pine trees. Bound to be easy to get in there. From shore it's a short walk."

"That sounds good. How about the safe inside? What's the make?"

125

"It's old. Take your listening device and listen for the clicking of the pins and gears."

"Okay. Give me a couple days to heal this bear trap wound and I'll get in there."

"Just remember to bring those pearls to the warehouse. If you see any information about how they have been making them, bring that too. There should be different colors of pearls."

"I'll be a different color if I get caught."

"Will be if you don't get caught and don't have those pearls."

25.

Marcia dressed in camouflage attire: a forested green and beige pantsuit with a long-sleeve tan shirt. She put on cotton socks and moccasins.

She grabbed a camera and her pistol -- stuck them in a pack with a water bottle, can of tuna, and some crackers.

If only the ants don't get to the crackers, she thought.

She got in the car and made the thirty minute drive to the rear of the Cloudwaters' property and parked on a side trail.

From what Rufus had told her, the cabin was a couple of hundred yards down a path to the west.

She saw the path and began to walk avoiding spider webs, which had formed around large clumps of grass

She sure hoped Rufus knew what he was doing with this plan to catch a stalker.

What if the Indians did not know she was coming and fired a shot in her direction?

But as time had gone on, she trusted Rufus with her life. There had already been a couple of instances when he was there for her.

And if he could guide a boat across the rough waters of the James River and take care of her for a whole day in strange territory, surely he had a good plan finding this stalker or jewel thief.

Rufus would be in church with the Cloudwaters this morning– knowing that if the stalker were to break in to the cabin – it would most likely be when the Indians were at church.

She tripped on some rutted holes in the path and reminded herself to think about steps over unseen holes and objects under heavy layers of pine straw. Fallen limbs were everywhere. Dirt channels made from torrential rains and over flooding creeks crossed along the path.

And there were lots of mosquitoes in this area because of water puddles. Fortunately, she had sprayed herself with pine oil and put a little Vaseline around her exposed areas to keep them off.

For the most part it worked, as she ducked down under limbs and brushed away briers in search of the cabin and oyster bed areas, and she did not get bit.

A few times she thought she had heard someone in the woods. Deer would not be rutting this time of year but squirrels could easily be rustling the leaves in search of last fall's nuts.

The noise then sounded like a pounding: she thought it was a hydraulic operated weight driving pilings into the riverbed as the sound continued to reverberate through the air as she walked.

Probably building a pier structure, or maybe its coming from the shipyard.

Fifty yards ahead she saw the cabin, which was situated between two tributaries feeding the James.

There were dikes fronting the tributaries and wooden channels running along their edges with a walkway in the middle.

At the end of the channels was a table and a sink; and an overhead shelter of slate shingles on plywood attached to 4 x 4 posts.

She looked around the perimeter slowly. All was quiet except for a few brown leaves falling from trees and hitting the ground every couple of seconds.

She looked for an area to hide; she walked to a brushy area behind the oyster beds where she brushed away pine straw, twigs, and some gravel. She took a large garbage bag from her pack and spread it out and sat down -- becoming aware of her surroundings and an escape route if needed.

Time moved slowly, as she listened for any noise and wondered about danger.

She made sure her gun was operable by loading and re-loading the chamber. She wondered about being spotted first, or if there were multiple stalkers. But no, she would not be scared: God was with her.

Maybe she should just take some pictures and leave and figure it all out later. That seemed like the best plan, but when a figure's image inched through the woods around the corner of the cabin from the river side and looked suspiciously at the front of the area, she knew what she would have to do.

He wasn't much bigger than her, but that could be a problem because she learned long ago that shorter people were smarter to make up for their height.

She also knew that she should have taken that judo class when the town offered it last week.

26.

Reggie Fuzman had swiped the gnats off his face and laid down the two oars he had used to row a 12' wooden boat to the Cloudwaters' property.

The oars were still dripping water at their ends as he swore he would never do this again – jail would be better than rowing a boat and sneaking into an Indian's cabin.

Even though it had only been a short row from a couple hundred yards upstream of the Cloudwaters' property, it seemed like two miles with the wind blowing against the bow and the tide flooding.

The last time he had exercised this much was at a gym with weights years ago. Now, a few push-ups in the mornings were the extent of his exercising.

After a small wave had come from the river, the boat floundered on a mud flat and stopped -- short of a bank with scrub brush that covered its edges.

Reggie looked for somewhere to place the oars in the water and push the boat forward but it was all muck.

Finally, he waited for another wave. When it came, he rocked the boat forward towards the bank.

The bow lifted up and touched land, and Reggie hurried to the front end with a rope and tied it to a small pine.

He brought the stern of the boat closer to land and tied it to the end of another pine.

He had looked at the boat with pride thinking he might make a good sailor after all, but then realization hit him that he had better hurry and retriev his bag of tools to find the Indian's cabin while they were at church.

After having studied a topographical map the previous day, he walked east along a small ditch to a large circle of oak trees where there was an open trail.

Just as he had stepped onto the path, a grouse lifted its full body above the earth and disappeared through the trees.

He froze with fear -- only to see the bird a second.

Regaining his senses, he continued up the path and saw the cabin's dark shadow through the forested area. Alongside the cabin were the water troughs with a sheltered area in the rear.

He looked for a back door of the cabin but there was none.

He silently cursed the Indians for not making two doors. *But what Indian would put two openings on teepees only to be in further danger?* He thought to himself.

He had walked slowly around the area looking for signs of anyone or an animal. A dog began to bark and started moving towards him.

He was prepared for the dog with a can of pepper spray and s leftover cheeseburger.

He threw the burger towards the dog and waited a few minutes. Sure enough, the hungry dog turned his attention to the burger and started chewing ravenously without looking at Reggie.

"Indians ought to feed their animals better," he murmured to himself.

27.

Marcia heard the dog bark and saw the grouse flapping its wings through the trees. And then there was the crackling of wooden branches every so often that become louder every minute.

The moment she saw him, she pushed a contact button on her telephone for Rufus until his voice mail responded – she knew he would know that there was trouble.

But it would still take him 15 minutes to get here.

She took the .38 caliber pistol from her bag and stepped out confidently from behind the tree.

She spread her legs shoulder length and said "Stop!"

Reggie froze in terror as he had his lock pick out working to get in the cabin's door.

He turned around slowly to see who he thought it was.

"Well, hello pretty girl," he said as he dropped his hand slowly.

"Take out your gun and throw it this way."

Reggie slowly reached behind him.

Marcia fired off a shot to the ground just left of his foot.

"Quickly, with your hand on the barrel."

"Okay, Okay. Don't shoot. I heard about you facing down three of Skooly's thugs last year."

"Yeah, well, four makes an even number for a resume. Put your hand on the pistol barrel and throw it now," Marcia said while looking through the sights of her pistol for another place to shoot near him.

Reggie tossed his gun toward the front of her and looked around for anything he could use as a weapon.

She kept her eyes on him and kicked the pistol further behind her.

"What now pretty lady? The cops won't help you."

Marcia stood erect, but she wanted to scratch her sweaty face from the mosquitoes and humidity. She resisted the urge to brush back her hair.

"Just need paramedics if you don't shut up."

Reggie looked around for an escape route but he didn't want to get shot, and he knew Marcia would do it; so he resigned himself to wait for her to tire of holding the gun.

"Sit down, now!" Marcia said as she relaxed the grip on her gun to keep the blood flowing through her hands and sweat off the handle.

Reggie said nothing but sat down and resigned himself to being arrested. The one positive thought he had was not having to row the boat back.

After a few minutes of silence, a crackling sound caught his attention to the right, and there was Rufus Stronger in his best dressed attire.

28.

"Missed you at church," Rufus said as he approached the group and looked at Fuzman.

"You know I don't do that," Reggie said.

Rufus reached down on the ground and picked up the pistol.

"Might help your disposition," Rufus said.

Reggie bowed his head knowing he was caught for good now.

Rufus had handcuffs available and opened them up with a key; he kneeled behind Reggie and put them on Reggie's outstretched hands.

In a few minutes, a policeman arrived and took Reggie downtown to be booked.

"Well, that's one down," Rufus said as he looked at the patrol car departing.

"Bigger than him, isn't it?" Marcia asked.

"You bet. But this keeps our pay coming in and Jim will be pleased. Good work gal."

"I get a raise for combat pay?"

"Did he fire back?"

"Heck no. I got his gun."

"How about hazardous duty pay?"

"That'll be good," Marcia said as she wiped her face and took a deep breath.

"Reckon how he got here?"

"Came from the river."

"Oh?"

Rufus looked over to the path that led to the river and said, "Let's take a walk. Nice day."

Marcia went back to her tree and gathered her pack of goods and put it on her shoulders. The last thing she needed was for an animal to come along and steal her bag that had valuables in it.

"Lead the way, Daniel Boone."

"You mean Francis Marion, the Swamp Fox."

Marcia giggled a little and said, "I'll settle for you big bear."

She had some feelings for Rufus, but in the back of her mind she was not ready to let go of her attorney friend Richie Granger.

Rufus said nothing but had his mind on acquiring a boat he figured Reggie had to have used.

He saw the oars first leaning against a tree – and ropes leading to the boat.

"Nice day for a boat ride."

"Oh no. I don't think so," Marcia said.

"You liked the last one."

"Yeah, well, the last one had a motor, and there was wine for lunch," Marcia said as she looked down at the old wooden boat and the water on its floor board.

"Maybe we could drag it up and put it in back of the Toyota," Rufus said.

Marcia turned her head towards him with her hands on her hips.

"Rufus. I know you like boats but this day is over. I've done my job and it's time to go home," she said as she turned towards the path.

"Okay, okay. Just a thought. Take tomorrow off."

"Now you're talking."

Rufus sighed and started the walk back with her to the vehicle all the time wondering who had hired Reginald Fuzman.

Stealing pearls was one thing, but fertilizing oyster eggs meant a person knew about chromosome activity and carrier cells.

A marine scientist, Rufus thought.

29.

"He got what? Caught by a woman?" asked Charlton Plover.

"Caught by a woman private detective," said Captain Tellis over the phone. "She's not just any woman – she knows the system and got Skooly to retire last year."

"Great. So we can't get the Indians to move, can't find out their pearl making process, and now there's a private investigator snooping around."

"Fuzman is in jail. Trespassing, carrying a firearm without a permit, and threatening a woman."

"What happened to your inside man who was supposed to take care of situations like this?"

"He can't work seven days a week."

"No, I guess not."

Part-time county commissioner Charlton Plover looked over his desk at the quiet waters of the James from his three-story plantation home and felt anger at the Indians. His family had been here since the 17th Century too, but the Indians started reclaiming lands that had been stolen by a paper genocide at the big building in Richmond.

All he knew was that his surname was on the original deed.

He too wanted to live beside these waters to harvest oysters and clams.

But the Indians had stopped him on several occasions – everything from putting large logs in the James just outside its tributaries to blocking his dredging equipment. Now they were putting traps around the perimeter of the property to stave off strangers.

Having 200 acres upstream along the James was not nearly as productive as the lower James for shell fishing – there wasn't as much tidal current.

Winning the commissioner's seat had not helped him: the Army Corp of Engineers would no longer dredge within a hundreds yards of any land owner's property, and the utility companies could obtain only certain right of ways on Indian land.

But the images of those lustrous blue, red, yellow, and black pearls had never left his eyes from the first time he looked on them in the family safe.

If only he could duplicate them, and he knew the Indians had the secret ingredients that were being added to the nacre to make shiny oyster pearls.

"You going to bail Fuzman out?" asked Tellis.

"No. Let him sit. And if I did, someone would find out about me for sure. I'll give you the money to get another person."

"Okay."

30.

When Marcia got home, she hurriedly got out of her ground stained clothes and went straight to the shower to wash.

Dirt was on her hand, arms, and face – where she had swatted flies away with her hands ·· hands that had cleared away pine straw and bark residue from the ground. *Next time I'll wear gloves.* She hoped she didn't have any bugs on her nor brought any into the house. The area was known for harboring ticks, red bugs, and fire ants.

While showering, she thought about the day and how exhilarating it was to catch a thief. *Maybe not a woman's job but I'm no ordinary woman. Not sure anyone is ordinary being a private detective.*

She dried off and put on some fresh clothes: a pair of light-weight cotton blue sweatpants and an off-white jersey shirt. She picked and dropped a string of wooden beads over her neck that had a crucifix at its bottom. The necklace had been given to her by a high school friend years ago when Marcia was maturing in her faith and attending a nearby Episcopalian church.

She dried her hair with a new towel and sat resting her body just knowing if she checked the home phone there would be messages she didn't want to acknowledge at this moment – no –not after participating in catching a thief.

My God. What have I turned into?

She smiled and got up to make some tea. It was Sunday, and she certainly would not weary herself of attending church this evening – she was exhausted enough.

Once she had her tea and thanking God for the day's activities, she looked over at the message machine and saw the light blinking wildly – and she knew it was Richie.

She had to face this situation about him.

She reached over to the telephone and called her good friend Naomi – who always seemed to have the answers for any problem.

Naomi answered with a resounding "Hello."

"Lord Naomi, Are you better after that sickness?"

"Doing fine girl. Where've you been?"

"In the woods catching criminals."

"For real. That your boyfriend's idea or you seeking new adventures?"

"No, no. Clammer and I are working on a case. How's retirement?"

"Nice but lonely, unless you count taking care of this terrier dog as fulfilling?"

"Well, you got that. There's nothing here."

"Uh-oh. You and Richie on the fence?"

"I'm on the fence and don't know how to fall."

"There another one?"

"I don't know. I do like Rufus, but he's my boss, yet corny enough to love."

"Ha. There you go mistress. Life is fun and adventurous – sounds like you got the best of both worlds."

"I'm not sure. Eight hours a day is enough with him, and I don't want to give up Perry Mason just yet."

"That won't work with men like Richie Granger who is moving out in the world."

"I know that. What am I going to do?"

"What anyone of your faith would do – front up and tell the truth."

"Yeah, over filet mignon and vino."

"Sounds like a plan. Come over and see me sometime."

"Sure Naomi. Thanks so much for listening – you're like a good mother."

"Be home by ten."

Marcia laughed and said, "Sure."

And then she called Richie.

"Well, well. The stranger is back."

"I know Richie . . . . But Rufus and I do spend time working, you know."

"On what?"

"Top secret."

Richie remained speechless – knowing Marcia would eventually tell.

"We're catching thieves at Jamestown," she said.

"Well, that's interesting."

Marcia told him of the day's events – from the time she had arrived under a tree stand area near the Cloudwaters' cabin to the time she got home.

And she loved being able to share these moments with Richie, despite any differences in their ways of living.

She felt refreshed!

"So you are off tomorrow. Can we lunch or shall we make a date for next month?"

"Lunch will be fine."

"Courthouse café at noon," he said.

She unconsciously nodded her head with a pursing of the lips and said, "Okay."

Maybe it was there she could break off the relationship.

31.

Marcia arose early the next morning and made her tea, toasted a bagel, and took one egg from a bag of pre-boiled eggs from the refrigerator.

Sitting on the couch, she felt confused -- but not depressed. No, not since she had a good job, money in the bank, and friends like Naomi.

Too close now . . . I'm too close to getting exactly what I want: a home, a good job, a little money. A full-time relationship can wait.

That was all she needed to hear. After finishing the light breakfast, she arose and headed for the bedroom to dress for lunch with Richie.

She hardly wanted anyone to recognize her though. After working in the court environment for years, she knew people downtown and did not want to answer any unneeded questions or attract any unneeded conversation.

She looked out the bedroom window and saw clear skies but a family of three across the street all had coats on and were hurriedly getting into their vehicle.

She picked out a white tee-shirt, a pull-over beige cotton sweater, black acetate pants, and a pair of low heel black leather shoes.

She combed her hair straight back and put on a wooden beaded drop necklace that had black onyx stones weaved between brown tiger stones with pewter separators. It was actually plain -- but dressy – and matched her black pants. And it matched her jet ring.

She went into the living room and gathered her clutch and car keys, locked the door, and drove to a fishing pier off the James River: to think about just what she was going to do.

The breeze was strong over the river and she took out a band to secure her hair while walking along the deserted pier on this Monday morning and enjoying the open river and the sound of waves lapping against the pilings. There was sure to be a storm coming, because she could feel low pressure hitting her.

She assimilated the feeling to her life: *This doesn't have to be a storm. We can remain friends! Lord, look at what I am giving up! A good man who is thriving in business, a good home, and security for life! But I would be expected home, having to cook dinner, going here and going there, and what would happen if I got pregnant!*

That was enough thinking as she reached the end of the pier and leaned over the railing to look at two ships leaving the James and Elizabeth Rivers.

She turned and made her way back to the car and drove to the café in Williamsburg content she was making the right decision.

When she entered the café, she nodded slightly to the crowd and found Richie seated at the rear.

She smiled.

"Well, hello stranger. Thanks for coming," he said, as he stood up slightly and motioned for her to sit.

"Oh, I've been so busy at work but loving every minute of it."

"And making progress with the Indians?"

"They really are nice people – just got some issues that need taken care of. It's crowded in here today," she said looking around changing the subject.

"You know how Mondays are at the end of the month with people paying bills and judges hearing motions."

"I do remember, and so I usually brought my lunch and sat outside on the bench."

"You like the outdoors, don't you."

"You know I do, and I look forward to spending more time outside."

A silence occurred between them as Marcia looked over the menu she had already memorized from earlier visits and knew she only wanted something light as a salad.

"Well, you look nice today and I was hoping we could do something together this week."

"I don't know Richie. I'm off today because I worked yesterday. I don't know what my schedule is anymore in this private eye business, but I kind of like it."

"I understand."

Marcia said nothing more as she thought that was enough for now. After the food was ordered and delivered, she ate in silence.

Richie looked downhearted, as he too was silent, knowing that his profession as a trial lawyer was probably causing him to lose the best woman of his life, but he would not give up his work.

After lunch was over, Marcia excused herself with a short "good-bye" and headed for the door.

She didn't know what else to do -- whether to feel happy or sad, but after all, her faith and prayers had got her this far and she was not about to step back from them.

And she was still thinking about that nut head Rufus and the beautiful home on the river.

32.

Marcia showed up the next day at work still a little confused about leaving Richie at the café the previous day: her emotions were mixed; yet sure of what she wanted and where she was going.

Rufus was already in the office -- in his usual attire of black nylon pants, navy blue pull-over, and brown leather cordovan shoes.

He looked up and smiled – still proud of his partner who had subdued a jewel thief with a gun and a surprise stakeout.

"Well, there she is," Rufus said as he put down the morning paper and looked at her. "Have a nice day off?"

Marcia gave him a "Why do you want to know look?" and went to her desk.

"Well, I did have lunch with Richie."

"And how is he?"

"Same as usual -- intent on representing innocent victims harmed by sub-standard products and interrogating product control specialists."

"That bad, huh?"

"Well, it's not a bad thing to help the disadvantaged but don't let it consume the personal life."

Marcia sat down in her chair and rested her chin on folded hands.

Rufus sensed there was something that had happened between them and said, "And you're not?"

"Rufus. I like my job and know when to quit. I may as let you know that I am not dating Richie any longer."

"And I thought you two were heading for the chapel."

"Well. The chapel door just closed, and how does one know when one is going to the chapel when one is always working and not yielding to the other?"

"You got an argument there."

"I don't argue Rufus. I am a private investigator who uses guns for an equalizer."

Rufus smiled and figured she was alright after all.

He said. "That's my girl."

"Partner Rufus. I'm your business partner. So what's going on around here today: watching shoplifters, catching jewel thieves, or reporting non-judicial conduct by policemen who should have been protecting the public?"

"No. We're taking a trip."

"Not another boat trip."

"No, a mystery trip."

"With wine and donuts?"

"No, no. Unless you want to. It's kind of a pleasure trip."

"Do I need to change again?"

"Sounds good, but no, stay like you are."

"Sounds interesting. Let's do it."

Rufus and Marcia locked up the office and went downstairs to the parking lot and got in his Toyota and drove to a spot of land on the James River just above the Cloudwaters' property.

Rufus stopped the vehicle at the end of a dirt road in front of a cottage.

"Nice place," Marcia said as she got out of the vehicle and looked at the pale green stucco building.

"Is. And there's the James in front of it."

"Let me guess. We are guarding the place for the weekend."

"No, not we. You are."

"For how long?"

"As long as you like."

Marcia stopped talking and tried to think about what was going on here, and thought, *No, I don't believe it.*

Rufus let the quietness ensue while a snowy egret flapped her wings and arose from a nearby pond.

A few tears came from Marcia's eyes as she thanked God for just being present regardless of whatever Rufus was talking about.

"Jim and Emma came by the office yesterday and were incredibly happy you found the stalker and had him arrested."

"Oh. That's nice."

"They heard the story about you and wanted to give you a small gift."

The day became even quieter with a few clouds drifting by overhead and a deer fly hovering over the

Toyota as they stood nearby. Rufus continued to look at the cottage while Marcia stood motionless.

"This is yours," Rufus said as be looked over the perimeter of the cottage and the trees surrounding it.

Marcia said, "You mean the Cloudwaters gave me this cottage as a gift?"

"That's what they said."

"There is one catch. They'd like for you to be observant to anyone coming down this road and chase them off."

"I think I can do that. Have you seen the inside?"

"Needs a little cleaning. Used to be a hunting lodge for the Indians, but it's functional from what they said."

"Well, Rufus. I don't know what to say. Well, sure I'll accept it, and thank you."

She came to him and gave him a little hug.

"Reckon there's an extra room for Rufus during hunting season?"

She looked up at him and said, "You bet, Rufus, as long as you cook what you catch."

Rufus just smiled and let her go and started walking back to the Toyota.

"Let's go to the real estate office and sign some papers; and then it's back to work."

"What about the wine and donuts?" Marcia said as she got in the vehicle and looked at him.

Rufus just shook his head and turned the vehicle around and headed back down the road.

Note

I miss places in the Tidewater area like colonial Williamsburg where my mother and I would walk along old cobblestone streets and visit Raleigh's Tavern, the Governor's Mansion, and the stockades. The Williamsburg Pottery Factory was also a great place to visit, with all its ceramic and plaster monuments.

Not far away was Jamestown – where I could look out from the shore and fort area to the James River and imagine the English settlers arriving on three boats in the 17th Century.

Across the other side of the river is a place called Chuckatuck, where a friend and I on a bored Saturday went swimming and diving for clams just off the shoreline.

I've hunted for game along the Chickahominy River, fished the Chesapeake Bay from its mouth to the Elizabeth River and north up the Eastern Shore. South, the Currituck Sound was also a great place to fish, along with the Outer Banks in nearby North Carolina. And I've walked the beaches from the Cape Henry

Lighthouse at the mouth of the Bay north to Ocean View, where I lived for years.

So I know the Tidewater area well, especially after working for the Norfolk Post Office and carrying mail and learning carrier route information for ten stations along with conducting digital training for all the cities of the Tidewater area.

I could only imagine Richard Lee, who arrived on one of the boats and made his home along the James River where he farmed tobacco and became Attorney General.

The Lees would make their way to Pennsylvania, Ohio, Wisconsin, and Iowa – where my father was born. He would find his bride on the Cherokee Indian Reservation, and after a ten year stay in Minnesota, they moved to Norfolk, Virginia, where I was born in 1953.

Coincidentally, I learned later I was conceived in Cherokee, N.C. when I found a postcard in my dad's closet after his death. My mother had written him from Cherokee in September of 1952, the month of my conception; they must have had a brief vacation, and she stayed there for awhile.

So maybe that's part of the reason why I am writing this book – feeling both sides of my heritage!

I lived in Norfolk for 37 years until I was forced to leave with a state helicopter hovering over me to the state line.

No. Not because I had done anything wrong – but because I was doing right and witnessing corruption in the judicial system.

I know how the Indians felt being forced from their homeland.

Tidewater was a wonderful place in the early years, with libraries, parks, and economic opportunities, but there were also some very evil people there. Sadly, the practices carried on through my generation.

Possibly he will show mercy to the people in spite of all the evil and idolatry taking place.

Decades ago, there was a little restaurant named Johnny Lockharts on Tidewater Drive in Norfolk, Va.

It was a quiet, quaint place, where my girlfriend and I would go on occasion to have a seafood dinner.

Johnny had an herb garden at the rear of the building, where he picked leaves and used them for food specialties.

There were no distractions in the little restaurant:
there were no cell phones, bright lights, big towers with
antennas nearby emanating harmful radiation through
walls and ceilings, and no beeps or answering tones
coming from another patron's wares.

It was quiet.

The tables would be adorned with white tablecloths
and lighted candles -- and situated privately within a
tall comfortable booth that had plenty of privacy.

I would look at the sparkles in my girlfriend's eyes
and see them riveting off her face and white blouse.

One can only hope for such environmental conditions
to exist again.

Many other people, such as the Indians, wish for the
same.